GREGORY EL HARVEY

DRAGONS MORE DECENT THAN MEN

A NOVEL

Books by Gregory El Harvey

JACKSONVILLE

Autobiographical
FACES IN THE SHADOWS

Serial
THE PATTERN OF A SNOWFLAKE
DRAGONS MORE DECENT THAN MEN
DRAGONS IN LOVE
TO DIE IN THE COLDEST WINTER
THE AUTONOMOUS ASSASSINS

This book is a work of fiction. All names, characters, and incidents
are products of the author's imagination, and any resemblance they
may have to anyone or anything anywhere is purely coincidental.
All places are used fictitiously.

Cover painting: *Purple Dragon* by Gregory El Harvey
(www.gregharveygallery.com)

ISBN: 978-1502438683

To Tai Ping, my best friend,
who died during the writing of this book.

ACKNOWLEDGMENTS

I am grateful to Myanna Harvey for critically reading the manuscript and to Cassia Harvey for helping with the publication process.

CHAPTER 1

Milan, Italy, September 2008

Margaret Swift-Jones flipped another page and then looked up from her magazine. Even the interior of the Milan airport could not suppress the lusciousness of the Italian summer. Certainly the promise had come true that if she came to Italy she would encounter a climate so beautiful that she would never want to leave it. She smiled to herself now and shook her head as she thought of going back to Vermont.

Then she saw Martina and Stanley coming toward her. For some reason, she felt particularly proud of them as they strode through the crowd. Martina's platinum blond hair and sunglasses were magical, her white dress and black shoes, seductive. Stanley, at her side, was charming, in a Russian way, of course, but charming. She was too old in this world to make heroes of people, and she took satisfaction in seeing beyond the mask, but somehow, still, of these two she was proud. She waved to them as they made their way toward her through the travelers already queuing up.

"You look relaxed," observed Martina, drawing up her carry-on and taking a seat.

"I suppose, dear."

"So, what do you think, Maggie, stay here for good? I told you, didn't I? Nobody wants to leave, once they get here. I'm not sure I want to leave, myself."

Having adjusted his wire-rims, Stanley offered, "It is time for us to go now, I am certain."

Maggie closed her magazine and looked up at the Russian, who had not taken a seat, she knew from experience, out of sheer anxiety. Often she wished to know more about the furnace that had formed this man. His mother Aglaya, living in Moscow, was still beautiful at eighty-one. She would give anything to interview her about the early life of her son. His father Aleksey, who died of liver disease in his sixties, had served in the Russian Army in the old days, the tough days, the real-Red Army days. She wondered if he would be proud of his son now or not, for although Stanislav showed his father's grit, he also showed his mother's sensitivity.

"Thank you, Stanley," she said, "for keeping us straight, but I am ready to fly." Then she added, "We don't want to miss our flight back to Siberia."

"It is not Siberia, I am afraid, as they say," he returned. "Compared to Siberia, Vermont is like Bermuda. You have no idea, as they say."

Martina grimaced, not at her husband's accent, but at his persistence in using this qualification. She stood, snatched the carry-on's grip, and breathed wearily, "Don't need to add that, Stanley, just make the statement, please."

"I love the way you roll the German eyes," he quipped happily. "I only said it to get you to roll your eyes at me." Touching the middle of her back, he added, "And now I have seen them. Now I have seen the wolf's gray eyes."

"Oh God, a knight. Maggie, do you believe this tender display?"

Maggie sniffed. "Hell no. He's hitting on you, stupid."

"I know this, you know this, and we both know that he knows we know this."

Maggie looked at Stanley, then at Martina. "Just tell him to kiss your ass, we've got to get on the plane."

Martina, slipping an arm around her husband's waist, said, "You heard her, mister Moscow."

He looked away. "You are both insensitive. I am Russian, I have a tender heart."

"Nuts," she said to Maggie. "They're all nuts."

Smoothing the back of her Presley-cut hair, Maggie relaxed as the plane surged past the clouds in its climb for the Atlantic crossing. She wondered why it should feel so strange to be going home. It was not simply that she must say goodbye to a charming Italy and greet a grim Vermont. Something else was bothering her, something she was anticipating. But life was like that, she thought, closing her eyes. It whispered in your ear as it prepared you for things you would never have asked for.

She smiled to herself as she contentedly listened to Martina and Stanley chattering away over which movie to watch. Even at almost seventy, Martina was undeniably gorgeous, with her pale skin, her German bearing. No one would think her to be out of her forties, let alone her fifties. She had been a good match physically, if not politically, for this Russian photographer she had married, ten years her younger. His years trekking through the snow alongside the KGB had left him, now at fifty-nine, with stamina. Martina had insisted to her that he must have been handsome in his youth. His hair was thin now, very thin, and his closely cropped beard gave him a rakish, almost criminal look, which the wirerims did nothing to diminish. She found him annoying at times, as did Martina, especially when his speech seemed to fill with what they called his goofy Russianisms.

She closed her eyes again. She had never married. Now, at sixty-four, she contented herself with the fact that men still looked at her, still found her attractive enough to want to sleep with her. What else could a woman wish for, she wondered, except of course for the man himself? Occasionally she found herself wanting no man at all. She and Martina, sharing a house for twenty years, had taught at the same public middle school. Martina had taught English, while she herself had taught history. They had been closer than mere colleagues could ever be. From the first time they met, each found in the other a spirit that truly answered to her own. For many years they enjoyed a very sweet life together. But then Martina fell in love with

Stanley, and with their marriage that sweet life was redefined.

Vermont

Through the cracked glass of her bedroom window Martina watched a squirrel emerge from the trash can beside the garage, a piece of bread in its teeth. After the bandit had made its exit from the backyard she lifted the sash, pulled the storm window down until it clicked home, returned the sash, and locked the window. She did not know why she executed this last action, for to the knowledge of anyone in the family Sophia's farm had never been robbed. When her phone rang she pulled it from the pocket of her jeans and without checking its screen opened it.

"Yes, hello?" she said, her eyes upon the trash can.

"Martina?"

Hesitating at the unfamiliar voice, she asked, "Who is this, please?"

The voice was confident. "Paul Kessler, CIA."

For once, it was not the Vermont autumn that chilled her. Then she asked, "What do you want, Mr. Kessler?"

"I would like to talk to you and your husband. It'll be a private conversation and quite friendly, I can assure you. What do you think?"

"What would the conversation be about?"

"About many things. I don't know how else to put it. But everything's fine, I just want to talk on behalf of the Agency. Would that be all right?"

"I will, um, talk to my husband, I suppose. I mean, it all sounds a little strange."

"Sure, I understand. I guess I can be a bit more specific. And by the way, nothing to worry about—it's all friendly and everything, really. We'd like you to come to Philadelphia for a meeting, a private meeting with you two and the members from your old team. You'd be coming as our guests, of course. Nothing fancy, you understand, but certainly as our guests."

Shivering, she asked, "Would Richard be involved in this?"

A pause. "No, no, I'm afraid not. Richard is dead, actually. He took his own life."

Although genuinely shocked, she could not find words to offer in perfunctory sympathy. It was as if she had at some point far in the past barred herself from ever doing any such thing should the occasion arise. At length she asked simply, "How?"

"He . . . he hanged himself . . . at home."

She closed her eyes for a moment, then opened them and queried, "His family?"

"None, I'm afraid, no one, he just didn't have anybody. But actually, Richard is part of why I'd like to talk to you. I suppose I can say it now, but I'll say it formally when we talk, I'd like to offer you an apology for the things Richard said to you. There were some pretty harsh things said, and I'm sorry for that. But we really need to have the conversation with both you and your husband, if that's all right."

She felt herself shaking as she replied, "Yes, I think that would be all right. It's fine with me, sure, but I'll talk to my husband and see what he thinks. I'll get back to you. Is that acceptable?"

"Oh yes, certainly, that would be fine. I'll wait for your call."

Closing the phone, she watched as another squirrel arrived at the trash can. But she did not entertain its activities, only imagining the strangled face of the man who for years had been her contact with the Agency. At first, of course, she admired him for recognizing her talent. He said she could read people, and he was right. And when he finalized the team, he chose her to be its leader. It was obvious that he believed in her and that she would do his bidding, and since he was the voice of the Agency, the bidding of the Agency. It was all a beautiful façade. But façades were like that, she thought, her eyes following the squirrel as it emerged from the trash can, food in its teeth. Façades were supposed to be at least more beautiful than what they covered. "Go on, little squirrel," she muttered as it scampered from the yard with its bounty, "it's yours now. Ignore the façade and feed your family."

Then she turned from the window and went downstairs. In the tiny living room, his face buried in freshly printed photographs, Stanley sat beside the printer, his brow furrowed with concern. She had seen the look before, so many times, in fact, that she now considered it to be an intrinsic part of his personality. Usually the look meant that he was struggling with some aesthetic problem, so that she could dismiss it as necessary to his photography. Rarely, though, it meant that he was struggling with himself in an unhealthy way, a self-destructive way. On such occasions, something deep within her, perhaps a sense of survival not only of him but of herself, made her think instantly that she must do something to rescue him. She had discovered early in their relationship that he was a deeply, perhaps pathologically, guilt-driven man.

She sank onto the couch as Maggie called from the kitchen that tea would soon be ready. It was all very pleasant, she thought, eyeing the yellow swirls on his new boots. The blue, finely tooled leather was just visible below the legs of his jeans. Recalling the intimacy of his love the night before, she imagined he was touching her even now as he frowned over the photographs.

"Why would a Russian," she asked after clearing her throat, "choose to wear American cowboy boots?"

He lowered a photograph. "This is ridiculous question. Because I like them, that is why. And I like them because I like them, what else is there to say? And why bring up, like you are using a shovel, my ethnicity? Please, show a little sensitivity."

"But you are Russian, not American. Why would you want to look like an American?"

"The next time we go to Moscow to see my mother, I will buy you a pair of gorgeous Cossack boots. You will not believe how beautiful they are, especially if you are wearing nothing but the boots, and you may be trusting me, you will not look like a Cossack."

"You Russians are always the same."

He laughed aloud. "And you Germans are not just the same always? This makes me laugh, this makes me laugh so hard. Besides, we are in America, so we cannot talk about ethnicity, except to say that everyone is equally intelligent and talented and beautiful." Wagging a forefinger, he added, "You are not being very American, you are not being very politically correct."

"But you're Russian, for God's sake. You came from the hordes. And the Cossacks, good Lord, they killed everybody."

He nearly choked. "And the Germans did not? And listen, we are in America, where it is always cowboys and Indians. By the way, how many Indians do you think they killed to get this farm?"

"You're not being politically correct yourself, Mr. Osipov."

"Of course I am," he returned playfully. "It is only that I am Russian, and Russians are insensitive, everybody knows this."

"I'm giving up on you," she said, pointing at him. "You don't know what political correctness is."

"It is a façade," he chuckled. "It is a fake. It is another mask that you Americans make everybody wear. It makes us all pretend we love each other. Oh yes, I do know what it is. We Russians have the same thing. We have the social lie, too. We say you must say such and such about this or about that, and we put pressure on you to make you feel small and stupid and criminal if you do not say what we want you to say. I know what political correctness is. It is the stuff you scrape from your shoe when you step in it."

"Oh yeah?" she replied, baiting him, for she knew he needed to say more.

"Yes, it is correct," he grinned. "I am the one being correct. I am not being politically correct, because I am saying what I think inside. This is not allowed. I have to say what I am told to say. The Nazis made you say it, the Communists made you say it, and you goofy Jeffersonian Americans, with your two hundred and thirty-five slaves, make you say it. You Americans, I think, are the best at forcing people to say what they are supposed to say, which means that you Americans are the most full of shit than anybody."

"*Of* anybody, I think," she corrected, furrowing her brow.

He waved a hand. "Whatever. It is what I am meaning, and you know what I am meaning."

"So," she queried, for still he needed to speak, "you think Americans are more politically correct than others?"

He grinned. "I think, yes. You are better at it than anybody, because you have your predictable TV shows. You know, where the black guy does the computer, and the blond girl is his friend, and the white guy pretends to not be politically correct. The script is totally writable by anybody. You Americans wear this phony crap mask better than anybody, with your phony diversity and phony respect, which is nothing but a freaking lie that you make everybody tell."

"So," she said, "you Russians don't have it?"

"Sure we do," he laughed. "All humans have it. It is the mask. The British have it, the French, everybody."

"But you've singled out the Americans. Don't say you haven't—you have. I've been listening to your ranting, and you have. You've said Americans are the worst."

"You are. You have the most tools to do it. You are rich, and you have TV, and rich TV with better, prettier programs. And you have a legal system that is sucking the breast of public opinion. And that means, and everybody knows this, that if anybody truly says what he is thinking about someone else, he is guilty of a hate crime, he is a criminal. So, he must lie, or be sued or dragged off to jail. So, he does what he is supposed to do, he says you are beautiful, you are intelligent, you are of equal value. He says what you make him say, he is politically correct."

"God," she said. "Are you finished?"

"Of course," he chortled. "I will say yes I am finished. I am supposed to say this, yes?"

She sighed. "Why not let's just have some tea and make peace?"

He grinned again. "Perfect answer from a Capitalist. And now you will exploit the peace that you create."

"*Capitalist?*" she blinked. "You're calling me a Capitalist? I'm probably more of a Communist than you are, for God's sake."

"I am not a Communist, Ms. Jung, Ms. East Berlin, I am a Libertarian, everybody knows this."

"My last name is Osipov now, not Jung. And it's Mrs. not Ms." And when he gave a shrug, "You've got a screw loose, don't you?"

"Maybe a little one."

"Or maybe," she ventured, "it's a big one that's just a little bit loose." Then she offered, very tenderly, "I like your boots."

Glancing down at them, he replied, "I am thanking you with all of my Russian heart. I was afraid that you did not like them, and I was starting to get a complex about it, I think."

She took a moment to enjoy him like this, then said, "Guess who was on the phone."

"And now I get a riddle. I love to do the riddles."

She smiled and then said simply and without emotion, "CIA."

He did not reply immediately, but waited for Maggie to finish pulling the tea cart in from the kitchen. A visitor might think her a servant, a possibility to which she gave little if any thought. He watched as she opened the teapot, inhaled carefully its vapor, then announced with an *um* that the brew had steeped to perfection, which meant that it was very strong, almost like Russian tea, as she often teased. After watching her movements, for she was a beautiful woman, as he often said, he looked at Martina, his eyes serious, and asked, "What did they want?"

Maggie stopped fidgeting with the teacups. "Who?" she queried. When neither answered she looked at Martina, "Who called, dear?"

Shaking his head, Stanley put in, "It was your people, your nice CIA people."

Maggie rolled her eyes. "Good Lord, Martina. What?"

Drawing her breath, "Actually the man said he'd been sent to kill us and wanted to ask if we could just stand in front of a window, or something."

"Oh God, very funny, dear, just hilarious." Then, giving her neck a little scratch, putting a saucer and cup together, and lifting the teapot, "All right, dear, just take your time and tell us everything. We'll wait, won't we, Stanley?" Slowly she filled the cup and handed it to Martina.

And even these moments, thought Martina as she sipped the dark tea, yes, even these moments of love and happiness were part of the façade. No one knew or really cared what was behind it all. She didn't care, herself. And then she told them about Kessler and the apology he offered.

CHAPTER 2

Philadelphia

There were only a few cars in the lot when Stanley pulled the minivan into a space and turned the engine off. No one said anything, and the silence was broken only when Martina opened her purse.

"I have to fix my makeup," she said.

The Russian's eyes were searching the grounds. "I do not see anybody." Then he looked at her. "But you do not wear makeup."

Maggie sniffed from the rear seat. "Come on, let's go in. I don't want to sit in the car."

Martina looked at the familiar buildings of the school. "How many years, Maggie?"

"Too many, dear. Maybe we overstayed."

Stanley adjusted his glasses. "I do not see your nice CIA people. I do not see anyone. It all seems to be very quiet, how do you say it?"

"Eerie," answered Maggie.

Martina closed the purse with a snap. "Isn't that just like the Agency? When you want to see them, they're nowhere, and when you don't, there they are, right in your face."

He chuckled, tapping the steering wheel. "Like KGB."

Then, without another word, as if on cue, but one which needed not to be given verbally, they got out, closed the doors, and walked toward the school.

Martina sought Maggie's eyes, then she reached out for her husband's hand, gave it a squeeze, and released it. "I have a feeling, Mr. Osipov," she offered as she passed through the door he held for them, "this is going to be very strange."

"I am having the same feeling," he muttered, following them into the building.

As if from the shadows, a man in a tan windbreaker and ball cap stepped forward to greet them. "Hello, I'm Tom. You're here to see Paul, right?" At Martina's mere nod of assent, he turned without another word and led them down the dark main hallway, not to the auditorium as they were expecting, but to her old classroom, where, still silent, he simply stepped aside to allow them to enter.

Inside, all the lights were on and the aroma of coffee was pungent. Immediately a grinning man they judged to be in his forties stepped forward, his hazel eyes bright, and thrust his hand toward Stanley. "I'm Paul, Paul Kessler," he said. "Stanley?"

He greeted each of them cordially, but made no attempt to introduce the grim man just behind him, who stood in a slouch, his face sullen and flinty. A woman in a gray suit tended a coffeepot that had been set up on Martina's old desk. She looked at no one, apparently intent on the success of the brewing pot. To the side sat Gretchin Wheeler and Bradley Hopkins, who seemed to be chatting. Waving a hand toward them, Kessler said, "Of course you know Gretchin here and Bradley. But come in, and please let us take your coats, and find a place to sit, if you like. I think we're going to have coffee." The smell of coffee was so strong that immediately he seemed to chide himself for having stated the obvious.

When they had remove their coats and the woman in the gray suit had reluctantly placed them on hangers and hung them on the coat rack Kessler continued clumsily, "Did you have a good trip?"

"It was pretty good," Stanley replied thickly. "And I love this country, it is so enjoyable to do the traveling through."

Kessler shot him a look, surreptitiously eying the coarse sweater, well-worn jeans, and cowboy boots, but then said, "Well, I'm glad to get to meet you all, finally, I really am." He also clearly took in Martina's platinum hair, her smile, her eyes, the fine white sweater, wool pants, expensive oxford shoes. In a flash he mentally photocopied Maggie's sleek hair, black cashmere sweater, expensive pants, and half-heeled boots.

"You all know each other, I think," he said awkwardly, and then, "except for Mr. Packard here, Mr. Leonard Packard. He's with us. Oh, and this is Ms. Kelly Connors. She's just doing the coffee—well, for now—I mean, today." Then, again awkwardly, he said, "Now, if I could have everyone just sit where you want. The desks are awful, but we have a few chairs. And coffee, God, do we have coffee. And there's cookies too, or something, I don't know. Help yourselves, okay?"

The woman introduced as Kelly Connors said nothing, but simply stood staring at them, her eyes colorless, her face expressionless. Almost robotically she began separating foam cups from a stack and placing them upon a cafeteria tray beside the pot. This done, she looked up again at the visitors. When her eyes met theirs she did not alter her gaze or attempt a smile. She was very beautiful. Her straight blond hair, exceptionally radiant, fell to just above her collar.

Everyone readily took coffee, except for Maggie, who asked if there was tea. When the woman merely shook her head Maggie said that she would just try the coffee, after all.

For a few minutes, until he saw that everyone had gotten some coffee and found a seat, Kessler, in khakis, white dress shirt but no tie, and thin brown sweater, moved around the room, his head down, brooding, as if unhappy with himself. Then, with everyone in place, he presented, like a visual preamble to his words, an elaborate cordial smile. He seemed to swell slightly, as if in preparation of presenting himself properly. Finally satisfied, he drew a breath and spoke.

"Okay, let's get started," he said, placing his hands together. "Mr. and Mrs. Osipov, Ms. Swift-Jones, Ms. Wheeler, and Mr. Hopkins, I greet you, *we* greet you, we welcome you, and we are very glad that you have agreed to come here and meet with us. I know it was tough for you to make the trip. I mean, those of you who made the trip. I mean, Mr. and Mrs. Osipov and Ms. Swift-Jones. Anyway, I thank you for that."

Here he stopped, and for some reason, everyone turned to look at Packard, who sat in an apathetic slouch on his folding chair, no expression whatever on his face, his eyes as empty as a ghost's eyes. Aware that he was being scrutinized, he produced a grim smile and lifted himself to be a little more direct in his chair. He was dressed in a plain black suit, white shirt, a tie that only a bachelor would choose, and wore simple black walking shoes. The clothes were obviously inexpensive and perfunctory. Upon the desk's writing top he had placed his black ball cap. His grizzled hair was short but not cleanly cut, as if he had cut it himself. His eyes were half closed, like those of a sailor who habitually looked into the wind. There was something very cold in his demeanor and the smile was totally unemotional. He nodded uncomfortably, as if to get them to stop looking at him.

Taking this as his cue to continue, Kessler announced simply, "Now we know each other."

Gretchin shifted in her chair and crossed her legs. "Look," she said candidly, "can we all just do first names?"

He beamed at this, then clapped his hands once, like cymbals. "Uh, yes," he agreed cheerily, "I think that's a great idea. I'm Paul, just Paul, and—"

"I know who I am," she returned dryly.

He beamed again. "Of course. Ha, very good."

Unconsciously then she wrinkled her nose in the direction of Packard. She was not sure that she was ready to call the ominous man *Leonard*, *Len*, or even, God forbid, *Lenny*. Turning back to Kessler, she said impatiently, "And look, another thing, why not just tell us what you want—you know, without the sugar and everything? I mean, I for one would like to know why you've dragged us all here. I don't have a lot of time for people who don't like me." She looked at him suspiciously, then at the slouching Packard, then at Connors standing by the desk.

He frowned, then was thoughtful. "Yes, well, maybe that would be best really," he replied, pushing his hands into his pockets and rocking a little from side to side. "You folks, not too long ago, just a few months ago actually, made up a very effective advisory team for us, with Martina as your leader."

"God, that's stiff," Gretchin interrupted.

The strain this remark produced upon the man was obvious. His shoulders immediately fell into a slump. It took him a moment to regain his composure. "You're right, uh, Gretchin, you're right." His voice trailed off, as if from the realization that she had put him down. He glanced at Martina, who placidly sipped her coffee; at Stanley, who looked back at him with suspicion; at Maggie, who returned his gaze without commitment. He did not bother to look at Bradley. Then his eyes returned to Gretchin, who sensing blood continued her attack.

"I mean," she said, "what exactly do you want from us? We worked for you people for years, very successfully, I might add. We sacrificed a lot, a hell of a lot. We even put our lives on the line. That's right, not every situation was without danger—lots of them were dangerous. And this went on for years. And you paid us nothing, absolutely nothing. You used us, and then what did you do? You turned around and called us traitors, for God's sake."

"I understand that, Gretchin," he offered meekly, for he could see she was not to be stopped. When she sat forward he pulled his hands from his pockets and folded his arms defensively, antici-pating her onslaught.

"And don't tell me about Martina," she warned fiercely. "Okay, so she fell in love with Stanley, or he fell in love with her, or whatever, I don't care. That's not the issue. People fall in love with each other all the goddamn time, face it. Love doesn't give a shit about governments or politics. So, they fell in love, and what did you people do? You condemned all of us, the whole team. You insinu-ated that we were traitors and dismissed us like we were something dirty."

"But I was going to talk about all this," he protested helplessly.

"You treated us like shit and kicked us in the ass, and now I want to know why you've called us here. And don't be stiff, don't be formal, and don't coat it with powdered sugar, okay?" Then she sat back and sipped her coffee, wrinkling her nose again, for the liquid had cooled and was no longer to her liking.

Slowly he drew up one of the folding chairs and sat down. "Well, actually," he said, "you've kind of stolen my thunder." He watched as she delicately scratched at the dragon tattoo on her neck, and waited for her to finish setting her cup on the floor beside her chair. He had not appreciated her appearance until now. The red hair, striking make-up, the white blouse, the jeans, the sneakers, all of it presented articulately an argot personality. Then he commenced.

"Some of this has to be a little stiff, I guess, because I represent the Agency and wanted to say it in a formal or at least serious way. Anyway, here it goes. On behalf of the Agency, I apologize to all of you, especially to you, Martina. I'm sorry, you were badly treated, all of you were. I'm sorry, we're all sorry. The Agency apologizes here and now to all of you. We hope you'll accept our apology." As there was no immediate response to this, he added, "I would also—I mean, on behalf of the Agency— be interested in hearing anything any of you would have to say about this or anything related to it."

After another uncomfortable silence, Bradley ventured, "Okay, what would this mean for us exactly? I mean, practically speaking?"

"Oh, just good relations," replied the other, finishing with a jovial nod.

Gretchin made a face of disdainful incredulity at this answer. But none in the group, not even Gretchin herself, needed enlightening as to the import of being on bad terms with the world's foremost intelligence agency. Being at odds with the CIA was nothing any sane person would savor, unless of course, there was a cause to be forwarded or defended. And even then, not even the most fervent crusader would relish such a situation.

Bradley said nothing to Kessler's answer. Instead, he leaned farther forward, his elbows upon his knees, and waited for things to progress.

Gretchin, rolling her eyes, still angry as well as incredulous, could only say, "You called us here to apologize?"

Kessler smiled helplessly. "Yes," he replied, "I'm afraid that's about the size of it. That's, that's about it, yes. And what does, uh, everyone say to that? What do you think?"

Stanley, stretching his legs out and crossing them to rest one boot upon the other, looked toward the ceiling, obviously lost in thought. He did not care much for any of it. He had seen so much of it with his own people, first the KGB and then the people that weren't supposed to be the KGB anymore. In his youth he had served the system faithfully. But now, since meeting and falling in love with Martina, since finding this love that seemed more real than anything he had believed in before, he no longer saw the system, any system, to be worth serving. All his life he had seen the Russians making a living by hating the Americans. And since coming to America he had seen the Americans making a living by hating the Russians. Perhaps the systems and their incessantly adversarial stance were necessary, certainly they were simply human and necessary. But he would no longer believe in them or serve them. He might work for them, he might enter the arena for them, but he could never believe in them or serve them or give his heart to them again.

Martina, her eyes upon the blue toes of her husband's boots, said nothing. Unlike Gretchin, she had known beforehand the purpose for the meeting, or at least this initial purpose. The cadence of her husband's breathing as he stared at the ceiling told her he did not wish to deal with the real world just now. And that was fine, she thought, he had withdrawn into his idealism of not being subject to idealism, and for her own part, she did not wish to woo him from that withdrawal. She loved him, she so very much loved him. That love had been the cause of all the problem in the first place. Loving him was not just chemical, she knew, but was also intellectual. She had not intended to fall in love with him, that was a fact. But when she did, or at least, once it had happened to her, once the chemistry had called her and then taken hold of her, then she loved him intentionally, quite intentionally. And now, what was she to say, how was she to answer this man, this representative, this ambassador of peace who had come bearing such an apology from the very government itself? She recalled the team, its birth and development, its full-blown work involving unwanted aliens, people who had come to the United States as societal infiltrators, people with ill intent. They were to target these people, develop a relationship with them, win their confidence, and extract the information necessary to incriminate them. Having been supplied by the Agency with only pertinent information, which usually included personal biographical data about the individual in question, the team developed a simple strategy and then went to work. Although every member of the team had worked successfully in developing relationships and gathering information from targets, she was held in particularly high esteem by the Agency, even considered to be a master of her trade, for she had never failed. Never, that is, except once. The target had been the Russian immigrant Mr. Stanislav Osipov.

"Excuse me, Paul?" said Maggie hesitantly. "These are pretty sensitive things we're discussing, or at least potentially are. This is a public school. Is it—"

"Is it secure? Of course it is. We've secured the building for this purpose alone, and only Agency people and you folks are here. We've secured the entire grounds just for this meeting. And we picked the location for its neutrality. Don't worry, whatever is said is secure, trust me."

Stanley shifted uneasily in his seat and asked benignly, "Why would we worry?"

Kessler shrugged. "I don't know, people worry. Maggie seems concerned. But don't worry about it, we're secure here." He looked at Bradley. "It's your school, right, Mr. Hopkins?"

Bradley cleared his throat. "I guess you could say that. I'm only the principal, but yeah."

Gretchin, cocking her head, quipped, "Well, Bradley, I guess you're just the horse's mouth."

"Lay off, Gretchin," he retorted. Then he calmly addressed Kessler, "But I'm sure everything's fine. I didn't even know about this myself. If you say it's secure, I'm sure it is, sir."

He sat back then, kicking himself inside for having included the term of respect. But then he considered that it might benefit him later on. Of the four members of the team formally dismissed by the Agency for their suspected complicit knowledge of Martina's affair, only he had complained bitterly and requested to be given another chance and placed on another team. He had denied any knowledge of the romance and had denounced Martina. But it had done no good, and he was dismissed with the others.

"Yes, well, I do appreciate the confidence, Bradley," Kessler responded.

Swallowing, "I guess I really prefer to be called Brad."

For a moment Kessler stared at him, but then said, "Anyway, back to the subject. So, what do you say, everyone? Will you accept the Agency's apology? What do you think? Yes?"

Bradley ran a hand over his crew cut. "I think *I* will," he answered. "I think it's actually quite generous of the Agency to do this, and I accept the offer. I mean, the apology. It's great. And I'm glad we can all do this, really." And after casting glances in the direction of the others, he said to Kessler, "I, for one, *do* accept the apology. Thank you."

Gretchin, sighing heavily, looked straight at Kessler. Momentarily she replied simply, "Okay." Then she gave a nod, as if to bring her own sense of finality to the thing, and looked down at the floor.

Then Kessler asked, "Maggie, what do you say?"

Conjuring her own image of a strangled face, Maggie replied thoughtfully, "I say, that if Richard were still alive and working with the Agency, I would probably not accept the apology. But as he is not, I will."

Gretchin looked up. "What about Richard? I didn't hear anything."

Bradley's eyes grew. "Neither did I. What happened?"

Kessler seemed to be hiding behind an uncomfortable smile. "Yes, well," he stammered, "as I told Martina on the phone, Richard took his own life. No one knows why. He hanged himself, at home."

Gretchin shook her head slowly and uttered, "God."

Placing his hands together, Kessler said, "And Martina, Mrs. Osipov, what do you say? Will you accept the Agency's apology?"

"I'm not actually quite sure," was the response. "I didn't use to be confused by life. Years ago, I would have known immediately how to answer you. For most of my life I had walked in a straight line, because I thought in a straight line. Life was always just straight and true, and that's the way I lived, straight and true. And then I met Stanley here and became totally confused. For me, our relationship was mind-altering, life-changing. It was like I died and went to heaven. So, it seems like I have to come back to earth to answer your question."

Bradley, shifting on his chair, cleared his throat and folded his arms. "That's a little over the top, don't you think, Martina?"

"Yes, I suppose it is," she replied. "And maybe that's because it didn't happen to me until I was sixty-eight years old, I don't know." Then she looked at Kessler again. "All I know, is that I will probably never be able to go back and walk the straight and true again."

When Kessler said nothing to this, Maggie put in, "That's very well, dear, but I think the man should have his answer."

"You're not going to say, Maggie, *it's only fair*, are you?"

The other shook her head.

Martina looked into the green eyes, then at Kessler. "I do," she said at length, "I do accept the Agency's apology, since they have apparently accepted mine."

He blinked, then said, "Yes, I remember. You told Richard you were sorry. He treated you unprofessionally, I'm afraid. Yes, yes, of course, the Agency accepts your apology, of course. Good. Well, Mr. Osipov, how about you? Are we all squared up, would you say?"

Stanley smiled. "I think so, yes."

Kessler cautiously returned the smile. "You sound hesitant."

The Russian pulled his legs up to resume an attentive posture, but his demeanor was unmistakably aloof. "No, no. We are square, as you say."

With a certain finality, Martina placed a hand upon his shoulder. Then he looked at her and placed his hand upon hers. He too sensed the closure.

Kessler gave a nod. "All right, then," he said. "Good. Okay. I'm happy." But as if to check himself, he said, "I am happy that all of *you* are happy. And now we can talk about other things. But up, please, everybody up. It is time, I think, for more coffee."

Immediately Connors, a blank expression still on her face, turned her attention to making another pot of coffee and then sprucing up the meager array of cookies. Watching her, Maggie whispered to Martina that the woman was beautiful enough for Hollywood and that she couldn't imagine what the CIA offered her to get her to make coffee for them.

CHAPTER 3

That wasn't so difficult, Kessler mused, as he made
his way toward the end of the hall. It was pleasant
to walk alone like this. He could think without
distraction, he could look out through the clean,
clear glass to the open air. Those people weren't so
troublesome, after all. Martina didn't seem anything but crazy, which was odd, he thought, since
the Agency had considered her to be so German.
Maggie—no problem. Bradley—bit of a dip. Let
him keep the car. Praise him. The Russian—kind
of funny, with his silly boots and his gloomy look.
Strange man. Really smart. He could be dangerous, might figure it all out. It'll be too late, though,
too late to save himself or the others. Nice people.
Too bad they had to be used and drained and
discarded, just to prove his theory. But that
Gretchin Wheeler—God, what a bitch, not just a
problem, but one to churn your stomach, sweat
your face, drive your mind over the edge. But not

his mind, not *his*. His mind was solid and fixed upon the task of proving his theory to the Agency.

What a screwball term, he nearly said aloud, closing his eyes with contempt. *The Agency*. What a ridiculous name for the group that nearly everyone in the world was expected to suck-up to. He closed his eyes again, wondering at the sucking-up itself. He did it, certainly. Only idiots did not. That was power for you, you simply respected it *period*. He respected the Agency's power, he gloried in it, he downright trafficked in the stuff. But the other side of power was prowess, and the Agency's prowess he did not admire. God, they were so numb there. They were so mechanical, so methodical, so stupidly professional, so organized. They were defined by their own perspective of order and propriety. How could they ever understand? His ideas weren't theoretical at all, they were factual. He didn't need to say *I think* about it, or use *if* or *possibly*. He could say *matter of fact, matter of fact*, at least to himself. He could use the verb *to be* as much as he wanted. Oh, he may have to prove it to the Agency, but not to himself, not to nature. Nature, all of nature, every little part of it, knew, just as he did, and swore up and down, just as he did, that his theory was fact. Yes, it was fact, it was reality, glue that held the universe together. Hopefully the team would survive long enough for him to demonstrate the truth of it all.

But of course, he was holding his breath. His fingers were crossed that Connors and Packard would be able to protect these people and keep it all together long enough for him to strut his stuff to the Agency. To hell with them after that, he thought, both of them. Psychos. He was lucky to find them. Where do you find psychos? Yes, he had been lucky. Freaky Connors, with her pathetic childhood. Frigging psychopath. Get her in therapy and she'd probably kill her doctor. And Packard, with his jacket bulging with guns and his pockets full of bullets. Crotchety old killer. But maybe they wouldn't be enough, he thought, looking out through the glass to the empty schoolyard. He needed another one. Maybe not a psycho, but someone with some real material inside. Maybe a cop.

Slowly he turned from the window and walked back to the classroom. Good, he thought, no one missing. Then he heard his hands clapping for their attention, his voice asking them to sit down. It was a role that he must play.

"There are other things to discuss," he announced pleasantly.

Martina watched as Maggie said something to the Connors woman, then came to sit beside her. "Well?"

Maggie tried to make herself comfortable. "I've never heard such a strong Irish accent."

"From the North?"

With a shake of her head, "No, maybe somewhere in Cork."

Then Kessler began. "Okay, everyone. This is great. Everyone have coffee and maybe a treat?"

"*Treat?*" Gretchin muttered softly, squinting at the term.

"Good," he continued. "Now let's talk. I have a proposal to make that's been on my mind for a long time—well, at least for a few months anyway. Simply put, I want the four of you, now the five of you, to be a team again for us. Not only that, but I have a particular project in mind for you to start with." Here he paused, obviously inviting a response. When there was none he continued, "I've studied your records pretty thoroughly. You had quite a success rate, I have to say. Your track record is impressive, and we would like to utilize your skills to the fullest. And Stanley," he said, turning to the Russian, "I would like to invite you to be part of the team. Now, I'm sure, you need to hear me out first. I know that, I do. So, don't say anything, just let me talk for a minute."

But Gretchin broke in, "You want him to work against the Russians? God, that's crass. It's audacious. But then," her tone exceedingly sarcastic, "I guess, it's really American too, isn't it?"

"No, no, it's not quite that simple," he shot back defensively, his voice filled with irritation. "And by the way," and here he threw a serious glance toward Gretchin, "I want your trust. I need it. I have to have it. And your question, Gretchin, which was really more like a charge, says you don't trust me."

"What can I say," she remarked, with a contemptuous toss of her head, "I'm human."

"So?" he returned roughly. But instantly checking himself, he offered a softer, "Explain."

"Well," she said, "I don't think you exactly trust me, right?"

"Not, uh, fully, no," he returned, biting his lip. "No, I'm sure I don't fully trust you, any more than you fully trust me. But with a team like this, there has to be a reasonable degree of bona fide trust among the members, anyone can see that."

Maggie, uncomfortable since he began, said, "but even with trust, Paul, anyone can also see that this is a pretty dysfunctional group. We just don't get along, we never have gotten along. And as far as trust goes, I don't recall a time when we all really trusted each other. In fact, I think we can go ahead and say that we mistrust each other. It's part of our dysfunctionality."

This seemed only to animate him further. "But actually, I read about this in the team evaluation reports, and you're right, it was obvious. And yet it was my idea to bring the team together again. So, the social dynamic of the team doesn't bother me. In fact, it's part of my belief that somehow it's essential to the results you've gotten. The truth is, your team produced the best track record of all the civil advisory groups the Agency has put together. Anyway, that's my idea, to sort of exploit the marvelous dynamic of your group. I really believe in you guys. And as far as the trust part goes, I'm only asking for intentional trust, not intrinsic trust. In other words, as long as you all agree to try to trust each other, that's as much of a commitment as I actually want you to make. Does this make sense?"

"Why do we need to trust each other at all?" queried Gretchin, running a hand through her hair. "Is the project dangerous?"

His eyes going to the red hair, "Actually, yes, it could be, yes."

Slowly she pushed a handful of the hair behind an ear. "You know," she said with obvious contempt, "this is all I need, a government that first slanders me, then apologizes to me, and now wants to sacrifice me. God, I am *so* flattered."

Recoiling, he pleaded, "But what about the apology? You forgave us."

Maggie smiled to herself as she caught a glimpse of the Connors woman rolling her eyes.

"Oh, I did," Gretchin mocked, with a nod. "Hell yeah. Which means you can't turn around and do the same thing again, right?"

Bradley slid forward to the edge of his chair. "But I'll say yes right now. I like the idea, I'm in, count me in."

Although Kessler seemed pleased and relieved to hear something positive, Maggie and Martina merely sipped their coffee, and the Russian folded his arms and stretched his legs out again. Both Packard and Connors appeared to be distinctly uninterested in hearing more of the proceedings. Packard, visibly pained, practically writhed at the prospect of enduring more of the conversation. Connors, who had taken to a chair, sniffed at a cup of coffee, which she held in one fist. Gretchin, on the other hand, nearly spat at Bradley's words.

"Well, why don't you just volunteer all of us, Bradley?" she hissed sarcastically. "After all, it could be dangerous and you don't even know what's involved. I mean, *seriously*? You know, Bradley—oh, I'm sorry, *Brad*, or should I say, *Mr. Hopkins*—I've taught in your school for how many years now, and I've never figured out who exactly was responsible for hiring you. You do stuff like this all the time. I mean, you're the frigging principal, and you do stuff like this *all the time*."

Bradley's face, which had gone pale as she started, now reddened. "No," he stammered, "I didn't mean for everything, Gretchin. I just meant, for the team. I don't know what the rest is yet, so why would I agree to that?"

Maggie, unhappily swallowing a sip of coffee, offered calmly, "Paul, why don't you just tell us what's involved."

"Sure," he replied hesitantly, "right. I will, sure." Then, straightening his chin, he proceeded, "Yes, well, let me lay it out for you just about the team—I mean, the team per se—just being part of the team. I know you're wary about the project, and you've got a right to be. I'd be concerned, too. But right now, I want to talk about the team. I've put a lot into this, and I want to make sure it gets started, or I guess *re*started, the right way. Martina, very simply, I'd like you to continue as team leader. You know the ropes the best. And, Stanley, should there be a problem, a disagreement between you and Martina, you would have to defer to her decision." He held up a hand. "Just hear me out. I'm not looking for an answer today from any of you, really, including you, Bradley. I want you to go away and think about it first. Because, if we scrap this project, there'll be others, and I really want to know if making this team work again is feasible."

In a quiet tone, Stanley replied thickly, "It does not matter about the team, if you are meaning about Russians. I will not work against the Russian government."

"I understand that, and I'm not going to ask you to do that."

"But even to work for the Americans at all is to betray the Russians. It is same thing. Just being married to Martina is betrayal, in their minds. And do not forget, they are paranoid, like you. So, the idea of me on American CIA team is ridiculous. The Russians will simply order me to be killed, they will send somebody. If they did not do it before, do not worry, they will do it now." He shook his head, chuckling. "We were both under suspicion, you understand?"

"I know, I know."

Stanley shook his head. "Under suspicion of the treason. Just to be married to Martina, that is enough. If CIA did not kick her out, I would be dead, that is all. And now, if she joins you again, then it is back to the treason. And you actually want me to help CIA myself? It is incredible, what you ask."

"Okay," said Kessler, nodding, his voice heavy, "I guess I'll have to tell you a little more. Let me just say, that this team will be unique. It will be in service actually to *help* the Russians. The job was given to me to put together a team to fight those who are trying to instigate Russian-American animosity. I just don't want to tell you any more at this point. But I understand that you are not an American," again he looked at the cowboy boots, "you are a Russian, and you will always be a Russian, I am sure. At least, I'm sure you want it that way."

As Stanley did not reply, Bradley saw his opportunity. "So," he said, throwing a glance in Packard's direction, "it'll just be the five of us?"

"Yes, that's right," answered Kessler. "Mr. Packard here is going to work on your case, but he'll be on the periphery of things. You might not even see him much. Ms. Connors will help, too, but not be part of the team. They'll just be there to help if you need them. I will be your contact. If for some reason you can't reach me, *they* will reach me. By the way, you will be paid, not a lot, but you will be paid. Martina, Stanley, and Maggie with be paid as full-time, Bradley and Gretchin as part-time, since we'd like the two of you to continue working for the school system just as before. It was a great cover. So, we're not asking any of you to volunteer for nothing. Besides being paid, you'll have the gratitude of your country."

Gretchin muttered, "Good God, like I need that."

"But that's a good thing," he offered sheepishly, "don't you think?"

She rolled her eyes. "No, I don't. I think if it was possible for my country to show me gratitude, they would have shown it before. I'll just take the money, if you don't mind."

Stanley, who had winced at Kessler's statement, asked, "Paul, you said *your country.* This is not my country. Are you offering me citizenship?"

"That's a good point, Stanley. No, we're not. We were going to, but we didn't think you'd accept it."

A cool smile. "You have done your homework, I think, as my wife would say it."

"I think we have, yes," answered Kessler, looking at the cowboy boots. "You know, Stanley, I have to say, we need your help in this project especially, but if everything works out, we'd also like your help in other projects. You will have our gratitude."

The other merely shrugged.

Kessler blinked, as if weary, but then said, "Okay, well, actually, that's about it, I guess, for now. I just wanted to get us to this point today. If we all agree, then we can meet again and I'll lay out the project. What does everyone say?" Following a general assent, he said, "Okay, good. Please talk among yourselves as much as you need to, and be candid with each other. I'll call you in a few days. If everybody agrees to the team as I've laid it out, we'll get together and I'll open up the project. It was good meeting everyone, and I look forward to working with you."

CHAPTER 4

Although the lodgings at the quaint inn just off Philadelphia's Main Line was being paid for by the Agency as a gesture of good will, Maggie could not find them restful. Often her thoughts were drawn to the peaceful life she had shared with Martina before the trouble.

"You have the countenance of a judge," Martina said as the two women sat before tea and magazines in the coffee shop.

"What?"

"You have a look on your face."

Maggie shook her head. "A look?"

The other shrugged. "I don't know."

"Then why did you say it, dear?"

"I don't know. Forget it."

"I don't think I can. What did you mean?"

"Well, you seemed to be blaming someone. You had that *blame* look on your face, you know?"

"That's coming to the point, isn't it? And who would I be blaming, dear?"

Martina rolled her eyes. "Me. Stanley. The Agency. I don't know. Maybe no one."

Maggie did not reply.

"You just had that look," Martina repeated.

"Why would I be blaming you, dear?"

The gray eyes blinked ever so slightly. "For falling in love. We had a beautiful life. Then I fell in love."

Maggie's shoulders rose, as if lifted by a wraith, and dropped again. Who is to blame, she thought, when the chemistry of nature comes in, like a plague upon the wind, and two people fall in love? The universe itself may be altered forever, but who is to blame? After a moment she asked, "Where is Stanley?"

Martina, shifting the table in an attempt to bring it to level, frowned. "He's sleeping, still tired from the drive. I told him the boots had tired him out and that if he had just worn sneakers he could've relaxed and the trip wouldn't have been so hard on him."

"He took that well, did he?"

"No."

Maggie smiled, if only to herself, as she gazed into the gray eyes. She wondered at the countless times during her life that she had smiled to herself in just the same way. But life was like that, it made you reflect, whether you wanted to reflect or not, just as it stood before you and danced and made you look at it, whether you wanted to look at it or not. For twenty years they had lived together in the same house, taught at the same school, shopped at the same stores, attended the same community events. In the evenings, they had eaten together, taken tea together, and then graded their students' homework together. And when the CIA had recruited them to work as advisors in the anti-infiltration program, they had thrown themselves into it together. The sheer camaraderie of it was what life had been all about.

Resting her eyes upon her friend, she queried, "Do you know what I'm glad about?"

Martina closed her eyes. "No. What are you glad about?"

"I am very glad that we didn't need to come back to Philadelphia."

The response was labored. "I suppose we didn't. Meaning what? I mean, I'm afraid I *did* need it. I needed that apology from the Agency, more than anything. It was closure."

Maggie nodded. "But we have each other, the three of us do."

"Yes, we do, Maggie, and I hope it never ends. But we're realists, aren't we?"

"Yes, dear, we are."

"Good. We agree."

"You know, for a minute there, I thought Gretchin was going to throw the apology back in his face."

Martina's eyes wandered over Maggie's hair. "She can be tough."

"I thought she might walk out."

"She had a point. Richard was a very bad man. Real swine, I think."

"Well, pigs are cute. They have charm. Richard did not have charm, dear."

"No."

"I think of him hanging there in his house."

During the evening, when the three sat in a restaurant for dinner, Martina said to Stanley, "I know what you're thinking. You're thinking, *Capitalists.* Am I right? If you don't confess, I'll tell the waiter and he'll spit in your food."

Maggie was horrified. "Dear," she said, "please don't say things like that. Spitting in anyone's food is contemptible and cowardly, and I should think that even referring to it would be below someone of your refinement."

The Russian shook his head, but did not divert his gaze from the menu. "Capitalism does not bother me."

Martina smiled and looked at her own menu. "Still, you were thinking what I said you were thinking, yes?"

"Possibly," he replied.

"But then," she continued, "how can you wear your cowboy boots? If ever there was a symbol of Capitalism, you are wearing it, mister Moscow."

"This is a good point," he admitted, glancing up at her. "I will consider it when I am full of this expensive food."

"Consider it now," she teased. "You're being inconsistent, admit it." And when he did not reply she hissed at him and called him a cowboy Communist.

Maggie held a finger up. "A Russian with blue cowboy boots is sort of red, white, and blue, like the flag, and is therefore very American."

He frowned. "This is not a point. The Russian flag is also red, white, and blue."

Martina tipped her menu in his direction. "Did I say I didn't like the boots? They're splendid. And now we can get you a little horse, and you can ride him around the yard at twenty-five cents a ride, that would be very nice."

"Capitalist," he muttered back.

Later, at a coffee shop, resting a leg on an empty chair and prying the lid from his cup, he observed, "We are happy, yes?"

Maggie smiled. "We need another car, I just want to let everyone know that."

"It is minivan," he corrected. "It is comfortable American minivan."

"The heater doesn't work, and winter is coming, is here, as far as I'm concerned. We need a new car now, or even just a newer car with a working heater."

He slurped the heavy coffee, as if to show his indifference. "We will use blankets, it will be fine."

Her eyes narrowed. "It's only the middle of October, and this is only Philadelphia. If we have to go back to Vermont, I mean, we'll freeze to death just riding around in the thing."

Martina shivered. "I agree with Maggie. New car, new heater, it has to happen."

"You are skinny," he responded, waving a hand at her. "You are both skinny, and you don't wear enough clothes."

Maggie laughed. "Who are you calling *skinny*? You're as skinny as we are."

"Yes, yes, this is true, but the cold does not bother me." He formed an O with forefinger and thumb. "I am okay even in Siberia. When it is cold

I put on the coat, when it is hot I take off the coat. We will be warm in this minivan with sweaters, coats, and a blanket. It is done in Russia all the time."

"Mr. Osipov," Maggie retorted, leveling her eyes at him seriously, "the winter is my enemy. I shiver here, I will freeze in Vermont, and I would die in your Siberia."

"It is not my Siberia," he returned. "I was there, but I did not live there. I lived in Moscow, and it was fine there. My mother, who is very old and beautiful, lived for a winter in Siberia, and she is doing just fine in Moscow. It is cold in Moscow, almost like Siberia. The winter is healthy for people. Russian winters are good for you. Russians live longer than Americans do."

Martina broke a piece from a cookie. "I think we need another car, two of us think we do, and I'm not ready for riding around in the car with blankets and hot bricks, or whatever, to keep warm. The car's shot, anyway, Stanley, face it."

For a moment he said nothing, then lifted his shoulders and slurped the coffee. He did not really care about the climate or the car. He had said that he could live just as easily with hot tea in Siberia as with a frozen daiquiri in Italy.

The next evening, they drove across the city to Bradley's house. Gretchin was there when they arrived. A blazing fire made shadow people on the walls of the stone-walled den.

"This is wonderful pie, Gretchin," said Maggie when the five were seated. "Is it from a recipe?"

"No."

"Yeah, it's wonderful," agreed Bradley, sitting forward to tend the tea and coffee. The low, rustic table seemed larger than it needed to be. "If anyone wants anything, I can get it for you," he offered.

Martina, gray eyes glowing nearly yellow in the firelight, looked at him the way a German Shepherd might look at an intruder. "We'll surely let you know, Bradley, thanks."

He assented to this with a mutter and sat back. He had intended to take the lead, at least for the evening. It was, after all, his house.

"So, dear," said Maggie, "what do you think about the proposal?"

Martina closed her eyes for a moment, then replied, "Well, they are serious people, we all know that, we worked for them."

"And we crossed them," added Bradley. "At least you did."

Gretchin stiffened. "You know something, Bradley boy, I've heard comments like that too many times from you. And you'd better watch your step. What goes around comes around, don't forget. And if you ever cross them and expect the rest of us to back you, I for one am going to think really hard about it."

"When would I ever cross them? And they know I wouldn't, so that's a silly thing to say."

"I'm just saying, jerk, you'd better lay off with the snide comments about Martina and Stanley. It's done, so get over it. The Agency has, and you'd better, too."

After a heavy sigh, Martina said, "They're serious people, and that seriousness comes with the territory—they have to be that way. They do what they want, and you hope it's for your good and not your harm. But really, I think we should get the opinion of this man." Here she put her hand on Stanley's arm and looked at him.

But Bradley, pulling his foot up to his knee, put in, "Really? And why is that? I mean, we're the ones who were on the team, he was just the target. So, why would you ask his advice about the team?"

There was a groan from Gretchin. "Maybe," she said, her voice strained, "because he might help us see our blind spots. Martina's right."

He rolled his eyes at this, but then simply sat back to listen. Now everyone turned their attention to the Russian.

Stanley cleared his throat. "I think you must accept the offer," he said. "It was a very big offer, I think."

After making a clicking noise with his mouth, Bradley said, "That's it? That's it?"

Maggie was not alone in her disdain for this man. In fact, she had never known anyone to respect him. She had given up wondering at the idiocy it must have taken to hire him as a school principal.

"Well," continued the Russian, unperturbed, "I do not know what else is going on with these people, but if nothing else is going on, it was a good offer. I think it is just up to you, what you want to do. You worked for them. Do you want to work for them again? It is up to you."

Gretchin crossed her legs. "But what's your feeling, Stanley, could we say no to them?"

He shrugged. "They are serious people, yes, but also grim, I think that is the word, yes, grim. They are like KGB, only more civilized probably."

"You're trying," said Maggie, "to scare us, right?"

"No," he returned simply. "But if KGB had made this offer, we would not be discussing it over coffee, we would be accepting the offer and then doing whatever they wanted us to do."

Bradley smirked. "There is no KGB, it's defunct."

"Yes," replied the Russian dryly, "I have heard this, too."

"Oh come on, get over it, Osipov. Putin's the only one left of those guys, ha."

Holding a forefinger up, the Russian replied, "I voted for Putin. I visited my mother, and then I voted for Putin. Now KGB is president. But I have nothing to worry about, correct? Since you have assured us there is no KGB."

His contempt nearly choking him, Bradley glared back fiercely. "Well," he said, "I'm sorry, but you guys know my view already. I want back in, and that's putting it mildly. This is a way for me to serve my country again, this is it. I wouldn't turn them down for the world." He dropped his gaze. "Look, you guys, I want back in whether anyone else does or not. It means everything to me. I believe in my country, and I want to serve it." He put his hands together. "I really can't believe you don't want to do this. I never thought in a million years I'd get a chance like this to be on a team again. They were finished with us, people, don't you get it? Absolutely finished forever. And now I get this amazing opportunity, and if you think I'm going to turn it down, you're insane. So, you'd all better get it straight, I'm accepting the offer no matter what the cost."

But Gretchin was ready with her response. "Well, I'm just about gonna wet my pants over you, bud, you're so goddamn patriotic. I mean, wrap myself in the flag and wet my pants. Jesus! You are so stupid, Bradley. They just want to use you again. Look where it got you the first time. They don't care about you or any of us, they just want to use us and then dump us. That's my opinion, Bradley, and that's thinking straight. But you—you've gotta be a patriot. Why don't you stand up right now, bud, give us all a great big Air Force salute, and then shoot yourself in the head. That would probably be better than waiting for what they've got lined up for you."

Now he laughed aloud at her, and when her face burned with anger he jeered, "You don't know that, you don't know that. Which is why you asked about it in the first place. You've been taken in by your own paranoia, Gretchin, that's all. What evidence would you offer to prove their ill intent?"

"God, you've got to be mental. You want evidence? How about what they did the first time, dumbhead?"

This exchange had become so toxic that Maggie felt forced to clear her throat. For a moment there was silence. Bradley got up quickly, walked to the fireplace, and began nervously to fidget with the irons and then to poke at the burning logs. They watched him, for it seemed that he hated them all. Martina gently touched her husband's hand, as she so often did when difficulties were encountered. Although she had all her life been strong and a leader, she took immense comfort—a comfort she knew she needed to see her into old age—in what she had come to think of as the *little touches*. For his part, he never pulled away or even found this annoying. Actually, as her hand would touch his, he often became more lucid. As he looked at Bradley Hopkins, now poking the fire with vicious strokes, he wondered at the wisdom of the CIA in enlisting such a pathetic man. And Gretchin Wheeler, possessing a nearly nuclear antagonism toward not only Bradley but the Agency itself. Who would ever want her to work either for the Agency or with Bradley? Finally, giving himself a shake, the Russian spoke.

"I think all of us might be seeing a part of the truth. I agree with Gretchin about the system, it is not to be trusted, unless of course it is trusted as being untrustworthy. The CIA is a system." Here he gave an exaggerated shrug and grinned. "But that is true about everything in the world, everything has a system to it. Every organization in the world looks at people this way, like they are either unimportant or useful. People are either seen as nothing, and so, not seen at all, or as something to use. But the system never sees intrinsic value in people. Even humanitarian organizations do this. It is *the system*, that is all. The system *must* be this way to serve the group, and if it *must* be, then it is like the algebra, it is an X on both sides. The system must be ignored, I think, or at least, how do you say it, worked around, you have to do a workaround," and looking to Martina, "that is it, yes?"

She gave a nod.

"That's kind of bleak," Maggie said. "But yeah, I think you're right. And it's weird, isn't it, that the system itself has it all wrong? It sees the group as a person, but the individual as a thing. And even we are referring to the system as though it had a mind and intent."

But Gretchin shook her head. "What the hell is all that supposed to mean, in practical terms?"

"It means," Stanley answered, "that I think you should accept the offer."

Bradley returned to his seat and poured himself more coffee.

Gretchin, chuckling a little, offered, "They probably want us to do something very dangerous, just my frigging luck."

Bradley sipped the coffee. "So what, Gretchin? That wouldn't bother me. I'll even carry a gun, if they want. That wouldn't bother me. And I don't care where they send me, either, I'll go anywhere in the world."

The Russian raised his eyebrows. "There are some places that I would not go to."

"I would even," Bradley continued, "quit my job and go full time."

"You are very enthusiastic," remarked Stanley. "Did you get your enthusiasm genetically, or did you learn it?"

"Look, Osipov," the other retorted, "I'm a patriot, okay?"

"Okay."

"And what are you, by the way? Are you a patriot?"

The Russian sighed, as if from exhaustion, then said, "Why do Americans think this word belongs just to them?"

"Well?" Bradley insisted. "Are you a patriot? Do you consider yourself a patriot? And I don't mean, of Russia."

"Whoa, Bradley," Gretchin put in, "take it easy."

Stanley then answered, "It is a good question. I am, actually, not a patriot, I think."

Bradley, who felt he had gained the advantage, quipped, "Yeah, right. But maybe you are a patriot of mother Russia, I'll bet."

Another sigh. "No, I cannot say that I am a Russian patriot. Russian patriots are more passionate about their country than I am, I think. They have your enthusiasm. I do love Russia, but I do not consider myself to be a good patriot."

With a wave of contempt, "I'll bet."

"But you," observed the Russian, "you seem to be very passionate about it. You have wrapped yourself in the Stars and Stripes, I think, is that not fair to say?"

Running a hand over the top edge of his crew cut, "You bet, Osipov."

"Most Russians are capitalists now, you know. Yes, they are. Just like, tomorrow, you will be socialists. And then everything will reverse again."

"I don't think so."

Martina had grown impatient. "We don't need a political discussion. We need to make a decision about the proposal, and we'd better make it tonight. I have a feeling we'll get a call about it very soon. So, Gretchin, you're the one with the most negative fire, it seems. Do you want to do the team again or not?"

Gretchin waved her hand aimlessly.

Maggie blinked. "Is that a yes?"

Gretchin closed her eyes briefly, then said, "Okay, . . . okay, I'll do it."

Martina looked at Maggie. "Well?"

The green eyes flickered. "Actually I'm waiting to hear what you say, dear."

There was a smile in the gray eyes. "I can't easily dismiss the effort it took on the part of the Agency to do this."

Gretchin looked askance at her. "Is that playing fair, Martina?"

Martina dropped her gaze. "I don't really know what my emotions are right now, so I'm unsure of my motivations. I have guilt, anger, you name it. So, I'm just going to say yes and take it one step at a time. We don't know what we're going to be asked to do. I don't think I am as God-and-country as I used to be. I'm a little more scientific or just practical about life. And since this isn't about an assignment but simply working as a team, for now I'll say yes."

Maggie looked at Stanley. "Mr. Osipov?" She loved to call him this.

"Of course," he replied, turning his gaze to the flame in the fireplace.

The green eyes met the gray eyes. "I'm with you, dear."

Martina smiled. "All right, it looks like we have unanimity, sort of."

Tucking a foot under, Gretchin said, "It looks also like we're going to have some help. What's everybody think of this guy Packard and, whatever she is, Connors? They seemed weird, to me."

A grim chuckle from Stanley gave Martina a chill. The Russian slid his cup toward Bradley for more coffee. Martina looked askance at her husband. Maggie crossed her legs. Bradley, filling the cup, said they didn't bother him at all.

Gretchin, throwing Bradley a dismissive look and then rolling her eyes, said, "God! Would you people please speak up? We can't make this thing work without input. Come on."

Bradley threw his hands apart. "I gave input, Gretchin. What do you think that was?"

"It was nonsense, Bradley. Everybody felt the ice in those two, and you're just being agreeable, which is not helpful. I want to know more about them. They're weird." And placing her cup and saucer on the table, she slid them toward him.

"Well," he said, glancing at the lipstick on her cup as he refilled it, "Packard seems pretty serious, I guess. I'm not sure about the blond. It was, like, she couldn't talk."

Martina merely cleared her throat, which meant that Stanley should say something.

"My guess," Stanley offered, "is that Mr. Packard is not exactly a translator, as it is said in Russia."

Maggie shivered, her eyes fixed on him. "Which is oblique for what?"

Smiling, he answered, "He is a gunman, which means he is a killer."

53

"How do you know that?" Bradley queried, his brow furrowed. Somewhat reluctantly he pushed Gretchin's refilled cup toward her, then sat back.

"Probably," the Russian continued, "he would not even need a gun. The KGB had people like that. The Irish woman is worse probably, very bad. She does not talk very much, because she is not an expert at that kind of thing, if you know what I mean. She is definitely an expert, but at something much more worse than talking could ever be. Probably she has a lot of blood on her hands."

Bradley put his head to the side. "But how do you know it?"

"I do not for sure, but I believe it. When I say *probably*, I mean it is a horse I would bet on. But actually, this brings up another issue to consider." He looked around at them. "You are not killers, anybody is seeing that."

"*Anybody can see that*," Martina corrected. "But what is your point?"

He lifted his shoulders. "Another *probably* that I am having is that the CIA people do not intend to use you as just advisors anymore. I think they see you as graduated." He grinned at them. "Do not feel bad. Companies always want more from their employees, is that not correct? I think they are intending to promote you."

Clearly unhappy, Gretchin returned, "And that means what, that they're going to ask us to kill people?" Then she ran a hand through her hair and reached for the teacup.

"I would not worry about it, but I would think about it. I think you could kill somebody, Gretchin, if you had to, but not without some cause, and I think the CIA is knowing this. That is why Packard and Connors are there, to do it for you. But also, they will be bodyguards for the team, I think."

"Well," she returned unhappily, "they sure gave me the creeps. Talk about spooky, soulless people. They may protect me or even kill for me, but people like that don't *do* anything for me."

Bradley snickered, "Yeah, but the tattoo on your neck doesn't do anything for them either, I'd say."

Her eyes cold, she retorted, "I would tell you to kiss my ass, but I have a tattoo on that also."

Eyeing the slinking monster on her neck, he quipped, "Another dragon probably. Or maybe a spider?"

Dismissively, she replied, "You will never know, trust me." And with that, she blew upon her tea, then sipped it.

CHAPTER 5

Two days later they met with Kessler again, this time at a center-city hotel near Rittenhouse Square. Gretchin and Bradley were waiting in the lobby when Maggie, Martina, and Stanley arrived. Connors was there, too, the same expression on her face, even wearing the same gray suit. She had obviously not been talking to Gretchin or Bradley, but stood by herself, apparently waiting until everyone showed up. Martina offered a smile in anticipation of a greeting or a handshake from the woman, but neither was forthcoming.

"Yous're here," she said simply, her accent so heavy as to make Maggie squint. "Lat's go oop."

She led them to an elevator, where she pushed the Up button, then stood in silence. When the elevator opened she strode in, held the door until they were inside, then released it. But when a man thrust a hand in to activate the safety light and the doors opened again, she deftly stepped into the breach, her left hand presented palm-out in silent command that he halt. Obviously in a hurry, the big man stopped dead, froze for a moment, as if startled, then backed up. Still eerily silent, she lowered the hand, backed into the elevator, and pressed the Close button, watching the man until the doors were sealed. Only then did she select the sixth floor. When the doors opened she closed them instantly, although obviously prepared to stop anyone else from entering, then selected the fourth, third, second and ground floors. At the fourth floor she again closed the door instantly. At the third she waved everyone out, then exited and let the doors close. Then she pulled a cell phone from under her suit jacket, placed a call, and finally uttered in a low voice, "Wuhr here."

A moment later, a door opened just down the hallway, and Packard stepped out to have a look at them. When everyone had gone in, including Connors, he stepped back inside and locked the door.

Inside the suite, which was certainly not plush, Kessler, casually dressed in sweater and khakis, stood to greet each of them with a handshake. Eight padded folding chairs had been placed around a coffee table. At the center of the table waited a single box of doughnuts, a coffee maker that had apparently just finished its brew cycle, and a stack of paper cups.

"Have a seat, please, everyone," he said, continuing to stand until they were seated. Then he sat, almost solemnly, as if to preside in an official way, folded his hands, and said, "I am so glad you've come. Now, I won't waste your time with a lot of talk, I'll just try to keep things brief.

And I want to let you know that everything's been approved. Actually it was approved ahead of time. You are officially a team again. Congratulations, it's good to have you with us."

Martina could not refrain from wincing. "Just like that?" she asked.

"Yes," he replied, producing a simple smile. "It's so, if I say so, and I say so." Then checking himself, he offered apologetically, "I'm sorry if that's a little abrupt, but I didn't want to waste your time. I called all of you, and everybody said yes, so here we are. And I don't think there's really anything else to say, except that you all know the ropes, you all understand the Agency and the way it does things. Even Mr. Osipov here knows more about us than any, what shall we say, *secular* person, right, Stanley?" And when there was no reply he continued, "So, I just wanted to get on with things. Here, now, have a doughnut, please. And pour yourselves some coffee, please. Kelly, the coffee smells great, thanks."

Connors, apparently searching her mind for words of response, said nothing to this. Emotionlessly, her colorless eyes perused the team one by one. Packard simply grunted and poured himself some coffee.

Kessler, after bolstering himself with a few deep breaths, began to blink rapidly and then said, "I want to show you something, a photograph. It's a little gory, so I apologize, but it is essential that you see it. So, don't be squeamish, okay?" Here he lifted a briefcase from beside his chair, placed it on the table, opened it, and then held to everyone's view an eight-by-ten color print of two blood-covered bodies lying on a blood-soaked bed. After a few seconds he put it back into the briefcase and closed the lid. Looking around at them, he soberly, almost sadly, announced, "Our project."

Gretchin, rolling her eyes, was the first to speak. "Good God! This is—I mean, at first you said it *could* be dangerous, and now you show us this." Making no attempt to conceal her anxiety, she gestured helplessly toward the briefcase. "What the hell *was* that?" She grabbed a handful of the red hair and dragged it to a dubious position behind an ear. As no one spoke, she queried, her voice subdued, "How was that done?"

"A knife," he replied softly. "But some have been shot."

She was incredulous. "*Some?*"

"Oh, uh, yes," he stammered. "But I really . . . just let me tell you more about the project, kind of explain everything."

But Bradley sat forward. "Look, everybody, it's just a photograph, nothing to get freaked about. Let's just listen objectively, okay?" And after receiving an appreciative smile from Kessler, he said, "But I do have a question, Paul. You said we're all on the team, but aren't you going to swear us in, like Richard did?"

"No, no," was the slow reply. "No, that won't be necessary. You were sworn in before, and that's fine, that's sufficient. So, let me lay things out. Please, help yourselves to coffee and whatever's there."

Bradley raised a forefinger. "What about Stanley?" he asked, looking only at Kessler. "He was never sworn in."

"Not necessary," replied Kessler simply, as if to dismiss the matter. "It's really not necessary."

"Why not?"

Blinking, "Because I say so. I speak for the Agency, I *am* the Agency, as far as the team is concerned."

Packard grunted again and slurped his coffee.

Gretchin lifted her chin. "But that's power. You answered by fiat instead of logic. The man asked you a simple question."

Flustered, Kessler looked at her, then at Bradley. "Yes, that's right," he replied at length. "Well, let's just say, I talked to you all on the phone about the terms of being on the team, and everyone was compliant. I talked to everyone individually, including Stanley, and I'm satisfied."

Bradley pressed it. "But what about the allegiance part, and secrecy? We were sworn to allegiance and secrecy."

Packard, who until then had been reluctant to look at anyone, gave Bradley a cold stare, then simply dropped his gaze, as if the subject of his gaze was not worth looking at.

Kessler only said, "Actually I'm not asking Mr. or Mrs. Osipov for either. I think their honor in the matter of their relationship with each other and with their respective programs speaks for itself. And that's all I'm asking for, their honor, and I'm sure I have it. And I'm satisfied with that. If you are not, Mr. Hopkins, lay it out on the table, please."

"Uh, no, no, I'm okay with everything. Just checking, that's all."

Kessler produced a strained smile. "And you, Ms. Wheeler?"

"Sure, I'm just fine with it," she nodded, placing her cup upon the table.

"All right, then," he said, with obvious relief. "Now, as to the project, Stanley, did you ever meet your contact?"

Martina, her eyes upon the toe of her husband's boot, immediately sensed his confusion, but said nothing.

The Russian merely responded, "Why do you ask me this?" And when there was no reply, he queried, "Is the project about the Russian program?"

Kessler opened the briefcase again, retrieved another photo, and handed it across the table. "Do you know this woman?"

Stanley looked at the picture, then handed it back. "Yes, I talked to her after my contact had called to meet with me."

"What do you know about her?"

"Who?"

"Your contact was a woman?"

"Yes."

"No, I mean the woman in the picture."

"You know, I—" He broke off, and Martina saw the boot move again as he asked, "Is this an interrogation about the Russian program?"

Then Martina put in, "Yes, because if it is, it's really unfair and, I think, deceptive on the part of the Agency."

"No, no, take it easy," Kessler returned, his tone as amiable as he could make it.

Stanley shook his head. "I will not talk about the program. I told Martina all that was necessary, and your people knew that part already. They did not know if I was in it, so they sent Martina to find out."

Gretchin held up a forefinger. "Correction. They sent *all* of us. I was there."

"That's right," Martina chimed with levity, "I seem to remember that you suggested offering him a piece of ass to get him to talk. Do I remember that? Yes, I think I remember that."

Gretchin squinted, as if to a rival. "Funny."

Ignoring this, Stanley continued to Kessler, "But you know about the program. I told Martina no details, only the things you knew already. And she did not tell me any details about her program. There was no espionage. I will not talk about the Russian program."

"Frankly," replied Kessler, "I don't want to know about the program. It isn't even in my biliwack. Someone else handles that. *Richard* handled that, and now someone else does. So, I'm not asking about the program *per se*. And I don't care about your loyalty or your politics. I don't expect you to become an American or be a Capitalist or anything else. But I'm asking you to tell us as much as you can about this woman without revealing anything more about the program itself. Can you do that?"

He shook his head. "I am sorry, but I do not trust you. You want our trust, you want my trust, but I cannot give it to you."

Patiently, Kessler took from the briefcase a single sheet of paper and handed it to him. "This is a copy of the first page of a police report. Do you know that address?"

"Yes, it is the same address where I met with the woman."

"Check the date at the top."

"Yes, yes, I remember the date of the meeting was the day before this. It was in the evening."

"The people in the photo were in the house, in the bed, the day after you were there. The police found them after a call from a suspicious neighbor."

"I—I do not know how to answer."

Grimacing, "Well, *anything* might be helpful. Um, look at these." He took out two more eight-by-tens and handed them to him. "I'm wondering whether one of these people wasn't your contact. They were both Russian, had Green Cards, and had been working here for some time. The house was a rental."

Stanley looked at the pictures, mug shots of the corpses, then handed them back. "No. I never saw them before. My contact was much different."

"Ah, that's great," Kessler said softly, clearly relieved. He put the pictures away, then placed his hands together, as if to help him speak objectively, inoffensively. "We know that the Russian infil-tration program is entirely peaceful, there's no question about that. But this woman has been on our radar for some time now. There have been two other incidents where she has left a bad wake. The woman is clearly connected with the Russian program, but the killings seem somehow not to fit with involvement in the program. Anyway, we're baffled. And we thought you might be of help.

We're not asking you to betray your country, just help us find out what's going on. These killings were of Russians, you know, not Americans. All of them were Russians, maybe involved with the program, maybe not."

Maggie queried summarily, "So, you want Stanley to reconnect with his people so you can send in the team?"

"Um, yes, that's right. That's correct, that's the project."

Bradley cocked his head. "How many others were there?"

"Three total, actually, a single man and a married couple. But they weren't killed with a knife, they were shot. And they were shot with the same gun, a Makarov, the East German variant." Then he looked at Stanley. "The point is, though, we're no longer talking about something that's peaceful."

The Russian smiled. "You are implicating the infiltration program."

"No, I am not," Kessler returned, shaking his head. "I promise you, we're only going after these killings."

"But you came after me," retorted the other. "That is what your team was all about. I was the target, and I was peaceful."

He nodded. "I know. And the Agency is still doing that. But the team in this room will only be going after those who did these killings. You have to trust me on this. I don't know what else to say, how to say it, how to convince you. I'm telling you the truth. And if you discover information that has to do just with the program, you can keep it to yourself, we're okay with that."

Martina laid her hand upon her husband's.

He looked at her, then asked, "What do you think? Tell me, please, what you are thinking."

"I suppose," she answered softly, "that you should follow your instincts. And I will trust you to do that."

Finally, he drew a breath and said, "The woman was definitely involved with the Russian program, because she mentioned my contact before I did. But she said nothing about anything outside the program, and she was definitely acting with authority when she said they did not need me anymore. My guess is, she has a lot of authority. I do remember she got very scared, but tried not to show it, when I told her that Martina was CIA. It shook her inside, I know, I sensed it. I can tell you some little things about the house, I was only in the living room. She was plump and poorly dressed, in used clothes probably. The air in the house seemed to have no oxygen in it, but was filled with cigarette smoke, very heavy, but she did not smoke when I was there."

"Well, that's a good beginning, sir," Kessler said. "So, I take it you're going to trust me in this?"

"I suppose so," was the reply. "But I must at this point qualify my involvement. It would be stupid for me, and for you, if I did not."

Having said his piece and so now content to listen, Kessler went visibly limp in his chair. "I agree," he sighed. "That sounds good, logical. Go on."

"It is very simple, and yet, it is complex too. For the love of a woman, this woman, I turned my back on the nationalism, the ideals, or whatever you want to call it, of my country, my motherland, Russia. I still love Russia, but I am no longer prepared to engage in that nationalism. You know, us against you guys, or however you want to say it. And so, the Russians threw me out, basically—at least, out of the program, out of their interest. This Russian woman you want to know about did it, she said I was not worth anything to them, and kicked me out, as they say. Now, I was not offended at that, but I am saying, I will not be on either side against the other side. The Americans want to destroy the Russians, and the Russians, believe me, want to destroy the Americans. And even those who consider themselves tolerant, whatever side they are on, probably find the other side irksome, at least that, you know. I think the basic people just want better business relations between the countries, but those in power seem to exploit this natural animosity. And they are paranoid about it, on both sides, they really are. A child can see this. Now, I do not mind helping you, you Americans, to solve a crime or to save people from being hurt, just as I would want to help the Russians do the same thing, but I will not engage anymore, you must understand, in helping one side against the other side, no matter which side it is. Okay? Now, if you still want me to help, I will help. But if I detect, I mean that if at any one moment I detect, that you want me to help you hurt or even spy on the Russians because they are Russians, I will not do it. I did not ask to work for you. My wife did not ask to work for you. The project you present sounds, uh—what is it?—it sounds worthy. It has the sound that innocent people are being hurt and somebody needs to help them. I admit this. You ask me to trust you. It looks to me, at this point, that I can do that to a reasonable extent. But reason tells me that there is very much here to be suspicious about. So, I will agree to go ahead and help you and work with the team, as you say, but I will go slowly, cautiously, not blindly or just because CIA tells me to."

Martina, waiting for him to finish, then said, "I am German, but my Germany collapsed and my family ended up fleeing from the Communists and coming to the West. I became an American and was very *pro*-America, and that was all wonderful. But then there was Stanley, and I had to make a choice. I chose him. So, I'm back to having no country. I also don't mind helping to fight crime, but I will not join the Americans against the Russians or *vice versa*. You spoke of my honor, Paul. Honor is my country, if I have a country. My husband is my country."

Kessler was silent for a moment, then said, "Actually that's what I expected and what I wanted. This is the crazy thing about it all. It's kind of my idea, but I want you two to be who and what you are. I don't actually want your allegiance in that sense of nationalism, as you say. This isn't the Agency's idea, it's mine. They've approved it, but it's not their baby, it's mine, and I talked them into it. I think you'll be more helpful to us this way, and I don't mean as against the Russians—I mean basically as crime fighters. So, I'm completely okay with everything you've said. But I would like to hear from the rest of you. How about you, Ms. Swift-Jones?"

Maggie rubbed the bridge of her nose. "Well," she replied, "My opinion about it isn't as strong as Martina's or Stanley's, but put simply, I'm on their side. In other words, if they're without a country, I'm without a country. I would side with the Americans, if it came down to a hard choice, and my guess is that Martina would, too. My guess is that Stanley would side with the Russians, if he was forced to choose. I do see what you're saying, though, Paul, and I think I might agree. I guess, what I'm saying in the end is that if I'm going to work for the Agency it'll have to be on Martina's terms."

He drew his breath in consideration. "Ms. Wheeler?"

Gretchin gave a short benign laugh. "Well, I think I can say I'm an American, but only because I live in America. So, push wouldn't have to come to shove, I'd defend this country because I live here. And I wouldn't have a problem working with Stanley and Martina. Any problem I would really have would be with the Agency—you know, trying to forget the way they treated us, the way they rewarded us for our service. I did not fall in love with my target, and yet I was treated just as badly as Martina was. Your apology was appreciated. I mean, I may complain, but it was appreciated. Anyway, I'm pretty sure I can do the work again for the Agency."

Then turning to Bradley, he said, "Mr. Hopkins, I think you seem fairly positive about it all. But I'd like to hear what you think. Any special thoughts?"

Bradley's brow had been furrowed throughout the comments of the others. "I'm strictly hardcore American. I think you know that."

"How about working with Martina as your team leader, could you do that?"

"I think so, if it's all under CIA oversight. Yes, I think I could do that."

"And how about working with Mr. Osipov?"

Bradley gave his chin a quick swipe. "I could work *with* him, yes. I would have problems working *for* him, I think."

"On an ideological basis, I take it?"

"Yes. But again, under the Agency's oversight, I'm certain I could make it work. We can work together, I think, yes."

"Well," said Kessler at length. "I am happy, very happy. Things went pretty much along the lines that I had expected, but it was good to hear everyone speak. And now I'm very, very happy. I can tell you, the things you've shared are inspiring. You've got charisma as a team, and I think you're going to do great things, exceptional things. Very good, then. And Mr. Packard, Ms. Connors, any thoughts?"

Wondering whether this last query had been a little optimistic, Maggie imperceptibly raised her eyebrows.

Connors, until then motionless in her gray suit, as if she had been a cast and painted sculpture, again searched her mind how to reply. Awkwardly she responded with, "Aye, sher."

Packard grimaced, as though insulted, but then said, "Yeah, I'm okay." Then, oddly, he asked, "You people had any training?" It was not a friendly query.

"Well," interjected Kessler, "maybe we're getting ahead of ourselves. We can talk about that later." Then quickly he brought his hands together with a pop. "Okay, folks, I think that's it. Thanks for coming. I'll be in touch shortly. Just stay where you are right now and enjoy the facilities at the inn. Talk to you later. Kelly, close things up, would you?"

CHAPTER 6

It was remarkable to everyone on the team how quickly the next few weeks were made to pass. Like cards on a roller index turned too fast, the squares on Martina's calendar became useless. Stanley only shrugged, as if he had already calculated the mass of the team against the narrowness of the bottleneck they were being forced through. Maggie could only remark that, for her, crunch time was never think time. Gretchin and Bradley enjoyed the sheer velocity of it all.

First, another meeting with Kessler revealed an odd turn of events. He had presented to his superiors a new plan to fast-track all the members of the team to a status of full-time ad hoc agents. None of the usual career-associated red tape would be necessary. Miraculously, he felt, his plan was approved and then even budgeted. The team was to be trained immediately and put into service.

Initially the Agency had insisted upon three months of intensive intelligence and small arms training. But when Kessler suggested that subjection to intelligence instruction could damage the delicate psychological balance of the team they agreed. Small arms, however, was mandatory. They were to be, in short order, sent to Idaho for weapons instruction, outfitted, and then deployed.

Of course, the success of such a plan depended upon the acceptance of the team. Since a complete career change would be necessary for both Bradley and Gretchin, Kessler reminded them that, should they agree and then experience a change of heart, a return to their respective careers might prove extremely problematic.

"I don't care," was Bradley's response over a private dinner the Agency had provided for the team. "I'm happy to serve. It's a done deal, as far as I'm concerned. I am more than ready to resign as principal and sell everything, house, car, everything, if that's what it takes."

"I love Coke," said Kessler, eyeing him for this statement. He leaned back in his chair and added, "Always with plenty of ice."

Bewildered, the other only grinned.

Gretchin, slicing into her steak and without looking up from her plate, said to Kessler, "What the hell does that have to do with Idaho?"

He sat forward a little. "But are you really ready to quit your job, Ms. Wheeler?"

Lifting her eyes then, she replied, her mouth full of steak, "Yes. I told you that. I only have my art and my apartment, and I intend to keep both. I have friends who will look in on things, and my landlord doesn't give a shit if I'm there or not."

"Thank you, Gretchin," said Bradley, "for the sensitive language."

She did not respond, but continued to chew her steak.

At Martina's query concerning the roles of Mr. Packard and Ms. Connors, the assurance was given that they would work with the team as satellites, not socially integral to the team. They would make their appearance upon request or as they believed necessary, for they would be monitoring the progress from their particular vantage points.

Gretchin smirked. "And that means what, they're going to be secretly watching me from somewhere as I wash out my bra?"

His mouth a little open, Kessler stared for a moment, then replied, "Well, I guess that could happen. I mean, you knew that, I think, Gretchin. You knew there'd be secrecy, lots of it. That's what we do. I mean, really, Gretchin, is it reasonable to expect you won't be monitored? We have to be responsible, you know that."

"Of course," she shot back. "I was just kidding."

Bradley waved a hand. "She's crazy. She's always crazy. Gretchin, do you know what? You're too insensitive to know when to joke and when to be serious."

"Oh, and you do, I suppose," she returned. "You're the all-American halfwit, for God's sake, Bradley, so don't tell me when to make a joke. I'll make one whenever I feel like it."

Kessler shook his head, as if to himself, then pushed his chair from the table. "Well, thank you, uh, everyone. Thank you for your efforts. We're going to expedite everything. Good luck. Glad to have you. I might see you in Idaho."

Then he stood, dropped his napkin, and left them.

Martina lay across the bed. It felt so good as he reached out and touched her leg. Although it seemed to her that since their marriage he had caressed her body countless times, it seemed also that he still cherished every contact he could make with her skin.

"You are beautiful," he whispered, running a finger along the crease between her buttocks.

"Good gracious," she muttered, her eyes closed. "That is exquisitely exciting, Mr. Osipov. Do it again, please." And turning lazily onto her back, she added, "Only this time, do the front."

He loved her to be quietly sexy like this, and instead of doing what she asked, he just looked at her. He had not seen many women who were as beautiful at her age. As a photographer, as an artist, as he considered himself to be, he felt privileged just to be able to look at her like this. He must make the most of the glories of it, before time began to move its eraser across her life in visible ways.

"You're looking at me," she said.

"Yes."

"And why?"

He smiled. "I do not know. Maybe it is just the chemistry of it all."

"That sounds very idiomatic, Mr. Moscow. You're getting to be quite savvy at the language. And what will you do when I die?" When he did not answer, she continued, "I am an older woman. And now there will be threats not only to my face, my body, but my life. So, what will you do when I die?"

"And why will you die before I do?"

Then she became serious and answered, "I don't know that I will, of course. But I do love you, and I don't want to leave you alone, without me to love you."

"You are right," he said, looking away from her. "We are not talking now about growing old."

She shook her head in agreement.

"This whole thing with CIA, we know what it is. We have both experienced it close to look at."

"First hand," she corrected.

"Yes, *first hand*, that is how I meant it. People may want to kill us every single day, from now on. So, what do we say to each other about that?"

She reached for his hand, then looked into his eyes. "Well, at my age, I'm not looking to raise children."

He smiled. "Tomorrow we go to Idaho, this little Russia, I think."

"But we go together. And we'll try to stay that way."

"Together as husband and wife?"

"Well," she answered, "I meant more as, well, just alive." But after he gave her an odd look she said, "You would not have agreed to work for them if you thought the Russians were involved in the crimes, right?"

He put his hands together thoughtfully. "No, I would not have agreed. But it is not the Russians. The Russians can be brutal, I have seen it. Not more brutal than the Americans, I think, but it is not the Russians. Something strange is going on, but it is not national, you know, the nationalism thing, as you say, I think."

She blinked. "Did I say that? I don't think so. But, yeah."

CHAPTER 7

Idaho, January 2009

The long, narrow wings of the Twin Otter, designed by de Havilland for just such a squeezed landing, seemed to reach out angelically into the darkness for more lift as the plane dropped inside the tree line and then touched down. As it rolled from side to side along the runway Maggie held her breath. When Bradley turned in his seat and grinned with a particularly juvenile delight, she closed her eyes.

"These Pratt and Whitneys are great," he exclaimed. "Listen to them. Beautiful engines. What a ride."

Gretchin shook her head at him in disgust, but Stanley, nodding and holding his thumb up, said to Martina, nestled beside him, "He is correct, for once."

"And I care about that?" Martina returned. "I think boys always love machines. It's that simple."

Amused, her husband replied, "Really? And the little girls do not? Not even nurturing machines?"

She looked askance at him. She usually found his sense of humor a strong point, but just now, rolling precariously along a dark runway in a plane she considered too small for comfort, following a flight she considered too weird for dreams, she could not appreciate it. Through her tiny window she caught the glimmer of lights as they approached the hangar. She knew that everything in her, all that was good and all that was bad, must now be focused incessantly upon the project.

"The project," she almost said aloud. What in the universe of reality was that? Why did she call it that, as if it was something positive they intended to accomplish, like a business deal? But actually, she considered, it was probably all more like sex than business, all somehow more against your will than because of it. Sex was like that, she thought, a mist you moved into against your will and yet somehow in your will.

"You are quiet," Stanley offered, looking at the side of her face. He wondered how many profiles he had photographed in his lifetime. Surely this profile, this face, this woman was the most beautiful. Surely also it was a trick of nature that he should consider it so. But life was like that, full of tricks, tricks that it was useless for you to resist.

"Yes," she muttered, "I suppose I am."

"You are thinking."

"Yes," she answered softly.

She thought of the small arms training they had just completed at the first facility. If she found it interesting at all, it was because of him. He loved mechanical things—cameras, engines, motors, machines, weapons. She smiled to herself now as she recalled how when they had first met he had given weapons the term *security gadgets,* exuberant that he had possibly coined the term. And he had loved the training, even the parts she found tedious. She had thought it odd that he seemed to know so much about the whole weaponry thing, the guns, the ammunition, the ballistics, even how to shoot someone so as to most quickly neutralize them.

As the plane rolled toward the lights she thought of death. All her life she had been taxied toward death, against her will, yet somehow in her will. It was as if the movement toward death and even death itself had been the great project of her life. And then the plane stopped completely and she heard voices outside. Spontaneously, intentionally and yet somehow almost against her will, she began moving up and out of her seat.

It was not until later, when she turned over under the sheets and smelled the skin of her husband in the darkness, that she began to think clearly and pragmatically again. She liked the way he smelled. Oddly, she had never been able to describe that smell, but contented herself in considering it to be pleasant and somehow comforting. She drew her breath slowly, as if to fill her lungs, her mind, with him. She needed to hear his voice and to talk to him. But she said nothing, for he was asleep.

In the next room Maggie herself lay awake, wondering why it was always so difficult for her to sleep soundly on the first night in any new place.

Reaching under her pillow, she pushed the gun farther away. Stanley had recommended always sleeping with your weapon. In fact, following the small arms training, he had taken it upon himself to add his own advice. His wisdom, he assured them, was not wisdom at all, but simply common sense. He had learned the ways of the KGB and knew the first common sense rule was never intentionally be separated from your weapon. When she scoffed, saying she could not see herself taking a shower with a gun in her hand, he had reminded her that she might not be alone in watching herself take that shower.

And now she reached out again for the gun and pulled it back to where she could easily clasp its grip. At completion of the Idaho training, she had chosen a stainless steel .38 Special revolver fitted with a soft rubber grip. The limited five-shot capacity of the cylinder had not concerned her. She had simply wanted something that would never jam. She had witnessed too many ramp jams and stovepipes to feel confident carrying a semi-auto. She had tried different makes and could rack them all right and eject and load a fresh magazine. She could clear a stovepipe or a feed jam, but knowing what could happen during the precious time it took to perform these tasks gave her absolute certainty that, for her, less was better. Five shots, always there, would be just fine.

She got up, slid into her slippers, went to the bathroom, gun in hand, and took a fizzy. At least, she told herself, they kept the heat up at night. Then she went back to bed, brought the gun up between her breasts, and lay staring up toward the dark ceiling. No, guns didn't bother her. She could hug one like a puppy. But gracious, those wretched little airplanes! Closing her eyes, she recalled the swooping drops, the indescribable sense of emptiness at having nothing stable under her feet. Now, of course, she would not be able to sleep.

"Just why," asked Bradley the next morning at breakfast, "is any of this necessary?" He had lowered his voice and was leaning over his plate of scrambled eggs. "This is all quite a set. You could make a movie here, I'll bet. Rustic. And the food's great. But why?"

Gretchin, beside him, spun her spoon on the table top with her finger. "I'm surprised you should ask. You know, draped in your flag and all."

"Hey, take it easy," he returned, scooping up a forkful of egg. "I can complain, when it's important. You complain all the time. I'm just asking, that's all."

Martina smiled. "What are you complaining about?"

"Oh boy," he sighed. "Nothing, really. What *is* this place, again? We can talk, right? I mean, this is all government owned, right? When's the briefing you mentioned?"

Now it was she who sighed. "It can be now actually, now is fine with me." She glanced around the table. "Is that okay with everybody?"

Stanley set his orange juice down. "Now is very good."

"What is this place?" Bradley repeated, directing the question to Martina. "You're the team leader, you should know."

"Why should she know, Bradley?" Gretchin put in. "She can't know everything, for God's sake. Think about it."

"And why the night flight? Where are we? Osipov, what do you think?"

"The flight was not long," answered the Russian. "I think we must still be in Idaho state."

"Just say *Idaho*, please, Stanley," said Maggie.

Martina lifted her cup, sipped the coffee, then said, "I don't know where we are. The Agency must have hundreds of these facilities around the world that they use for all kinds of things, training, recuperation, briefings, whatever. And they probably wouldn't want the location advertised. Maybe not top secret, but *you know*. Anyway, Paul said I was to brief you when we got here. I can tell you, the briefing has to be short, because I don't know much myself. He said we should talk about anything we wanted to and feel free to voice concerns, whatever. So, explore, take a walk or just sit around, whatever you want. They'll let us know about one day before we go. And then—we go."

"Ominous," said Bradley. And when Gretchin shot him an unhappy look, he said, "I'm just anxious to get started with things." Then brightening, "Hey, this place is really rural, isn't it."

Gretchin gave him a look. "God, you're a child sometimes."

"Okay," Maggie said quickly, "let's go over things. Could we do that, dear, please."

Martina smiled. "Thank you, Maggie. Yes, all right. This is sort of a rundown of who we are and what we do. The Agency sees us as a potentially valuable team and is willing to invest in us, at least to this point. My own reasoning is that their interest is fueled by Paul's theory and our old track record as advisors. A component of Paul's theory seems to be that a team like ours can sometimes be more believable and creative, when controlled of course, than a fully trained team of professional agents. Some stupid things may happen, and probably will, but in certain circumstances, with a little bit of luck, better results might be achieved. He has seen many highly trained people screw up because their perspective was too intentional, too focused, too technical, etcetera."

The Russian nodded that he agreed. "I think they are going to push us into pool to see if we will swim. Of course, Connors and Packard, who are certainly not novices, will be there. It would not be good if we all drowned at once, yes?"

Maggie replied, "How comforting. You should work for public relations."

"Yeah," said Bradley, "but he's probably right."

"What about the project itself?" she queried, looking to Martina.

"It's in the dark right now," was the answer. "They don't want to give us too much information."

"Yeah," laughed Bradley, "we might think too much and teach ourselves to swim."

"Well," she continued, "they want us to think more creatively and be less focused than if we had, say, a huge amount of information. We can be negative about this, but we don't have to be. Paul's theory is interesting."

"But," observed Stanley, "you said to voice our concerns. One concern that I am having is about the *stupid things* you mentioned that might happen. These stupid things might be illegal, correct?"

"Of course. But they seem willing to take that chance."

Bradley put his hands behind his head. "*I* think we get along pretty well. I think we do a good job."

Gretchin smirked, "We should have just asked *you,* then."

Pretending to ignore her, he sighed and drummed his fingers on the table.

"All right," Martina continued, "we need to talk about a cover. If a cover is needed, the Agency wants us to go just as who we are. Gretchin is an artist, retired from teaching in the public schools. Maggie, the same, a retired teacher."

"History teacher, dear."

"Yes, history, which might prove valuable. But your interests can be travel and photography, like before. Oh, those Bermuda pictures."

"You wore a string bikini, dear."

Bradley grinned. "Uh-oh."

Martina ignored him. "Bradley is only what he is, a retired school principal."

He snickered. "And my interests?"

"Whatever you want them to be," she answered without bothering to disguise her impatience. "That's the way the Agency wants it, natural, meaning that you can make it up as you go along. But they want us to be more true and real than fantastic. People are suspicious, they catch you at things. So, I'd say, whatever your true interests are, stick to those. What would you say your interests are, Mr. Hopkins?"

With a chuckle, "Good grief, it's *Mr. Hopkins,* is it? How many years was it? I was the principal, you taught at *my* school, and I never got *Mr. Hopkins,* I just got *Bradley.* It couldn't even be *Brad,* which is what I like, it had to be *Bradley,* like I was a kid, one of your students. I mean, you actually worked for me, and you treated me like one of your students, Martina. I mean, what was that?"

"I didn't really intend respect just now, Bradley," she replied.

Flushing at this, he pushed away from the table and brought his foot to his knee.

"Although, I do think," she continued, "respect is always better than disrespect in the dynamics of a team like this."

Stanley gulped his coffee. "So, I am to be what I was before, a photographer, but more like hobbyist? And I am probably to make that fit with current project?"

"That's right. And they want us to think of it always as a project rather than an assignment. They want it to be more creative than responsive. . . . So, Bradley, what *are* your interests, would you say?"

"Corvettes," suggested Gretchin sarcastically, "engines, football, flags."

He puffed his cheeks. "I don't know, Martina. I guess I do like cars a lot. And yes," to Gretchin, "flags. I'm proud of being an American, I like it. But as part of the team, I don't know. I guess, just liking cars, machines. You know. How's that? I mean, they have cars everywhere. I could just be a car and airplane enthusiast."

She smiled, as if to reward him. "Yes, good, perfect."

"And you, dear?" queried Maggie.

"Good question. I'm just a retired English teacher, and I follow my husband's photography."

Maggie blinked. "Charming, dear. And you could be his model too."

"Yes," added Gretchin, "his nude model, his muse. You could be mine too, except that I would prefer Stanley, I think."

"Yes, I remember. Do you remember that, Stanley?"

"I do, yes," he answered, reaching for a piece of toast.

Sliding her chair back, Martina said, "Back to the subject, I will say this, a comment Paul made to me seemed a little odd. He said not to be afraid to use our weapons. The way he said it bothered me. It seemed to be a kind of warning that the Agency intends to use us in—" here she looked at Gretchin, "dangerous situations."

"I knew it," muttered Gretchin. "I knew all of this team stuff involved weapons. I knew it. When Paul first showed us those photographs, I knew what they had in mind. And I knew Stanley was right when he warned us. He knows. He's been around those people. They seem to always want to suck you into using a gun. Yeah, I knew it. I could've told Paul no, and probably still can. But I think I'm okay with it. Let's just say I'm okay with it for now."

Martina took up her coffee. "I noticed, Gretchin, during the small arms training that you seemed to know something about handguns."

A nod of affirmation. "Everybody in the family pretty much knew how to use the Luger."

"Sorry, Gretchin."

"Sure. I struggle with it. I'm an artist. I don't like guns at all, any of them. I like paint brushes and a quiet studio, and maybe a museum or two. You know, the spiritual thing. I want to discover and build, not find and destroy. I dislike guns because they seem so negative. You have to work intellectually to see them as positive. And I can do that, I can see a gun as a tool that I might have no choice but to use. I struggle with the thought of using one, there's no question about that. But I think I'm okay with it. I see the need, and I will use it."

"But," said Bradley, "without hesitation?"

"Without hesitation? Probably not. . . . But with my luck, I'll probably end up having to blow some fucker's brains out."

"Okay," said Bradley, "enough sap. Osipov, why'd you pick a goofy Makarov, because it was Russian?"

A shrug. "Maybe I picked it because I am a photographer. Maybe I do not know very much about guns."

After a chuckle, "And your backup, the Tokarev?"

"It is not a backup. The KGB used it to shoot through cars."

Maggie groaned. "Lovely."

Bradley scratched his head. "But why the Makarov?"

The Russian looked at him, then replied, "It was known as death gun."

Bradley slapped his knee. "You just can't get away from the Kremlin, can you? I'll bet even that Connors girl has a bigger gun than a Makarov."

"Well," put in Martina, "we don't know that, because we haven't seen her. And I don't expect to, unless the need arises. And then, I can just imagine."

Bradley gave the table a tap. "Yeah," he said with a chuckle, "she's not the cook. I saw the cook, she's really fat."

"And Connors," said Gretchin, "isn't fat, is she, Bradley? You noticed that, didn't you?"

"Yeah. Who didn't? Hey, and I wonder what that Packard guy carries. We haven't seen him either. Probably a magnum."

Clearing her throat, Maggie suggested, "Maybe getting back to what we're doing here would be good. So, dear, one day's notice?"

Martina nodded, waited for a moment, then said, "Okay, I think that's all, everybody. I'll pass along whatever I hear. But for now, we are here. Let's all look around, explore, you know. There's a shooting range, I understand, and there are horses to ride, and there's a stream behind the trees."

"It's Idaho, winter, dear," Maggie said with a shiver. "Did you see the snow?"

"They said it wasn't deep, just a light coating."

"But I hate the cold, dear. All the world knows that."

Gretchin sniffed. "You're not alone, Maggie. It's cold as hell outside."

Then Martina got up. "Well, do what you want. Read, if you want. And I think that's the key, doing what we want to. They brought us here to loosen us up, not to make us tight. But I would suggest that everybody visit the range at least once a day."

"That won't be difficult for me," returned Bradley, "with free ammunition and targets and all. Hey, Osipov, bring your Makarov."

CHAPTER 8

For most of January and part of February the team kept close to the main buildings of what they had come to call the ranch. Each week, the Twin Otter would descend rapidly at the tree line and land, apparently bringing supplies. The weather remained stable, delivering only another inch or so of snow. But temperatures dropped steadily until they ranged from about ten above during daylight hours to nearly ten below at night. It was not uncommon to see parkas and lined gloves worn inside as well as outside.

"The fashion here isn't exactly Parisian," quipped Maggie. "The very cut of a parka seems to offend me. What is it, do you think, dear?"

"Perhaps the puffiness of a parka? For myself, I do not like nylon. One might as well dress in a plastic trash bag."

"We agree. We always did."

"Wool," said Martina. "Long woolen coats. You can line them if you like, that would be fine with me. But God, Maggie, nylon, it is so wretchedly artificial and ugly."

"Parkas are warm, you have to admit that."

"They are. And waterproof, or water resistant, which is it, exactly?"

"Well, now, dear, I think you'll just have to check the tag. And you'll want to know, of course, you can't wait until you're halfway up Everest to find out."

"No, certainly, one has to be ready for the elements. And there, Maggie, look, there goes another one. Is that man salting the runway? His parka's so fashionable, isn't it? Like a big blue balloon."

"Two balloons."

"Oh, yes, Maggie, that's right, the hood, the puffy hood. Didn't you always want to wear a balloon around your body and a balloon around your head? Coco Chanel, eat your heart out."

It could not be said that Stanley and Bradley had become chums, but their general gun talk and daily visits to the range seemed to be decreasing the ideological expanse that separated them. The Russian had not fired a .45 before, and Bradley had not fired a Makarov or a Tokarev. They juggled ammunition, shot blindfolded, and shared war jokes.

"Who is at the center of your dartboard, Osipov?" Bradley demanded one sunny afternoon as he snapped a fresh magazine into place.

"I do not throw darts."

"But who would be there, if you did?"

"Reagan, I am supposing. And how about your dartboard?"

Bradley looked downrange at the target. "Well, now, Osipov, I'll tell you. I rotate mine, and I'd need a computer to remember them all. There's Stalin, there's Khrushchev, there's Mao, there's Uncle Ho. Ah, but there's so many of them, I just can't remember them all."

Then he leveled up and emptied the gun downrange.

On another day, under a sky as bleak as any over an old East Berlin checkpoint, they traded weapons. The Russian removed his gloves, then pulled the Tokarev from its small-of-the-back holster and handed it over.

"Here, comrade," he offered. "Try this gun on for size. Is that the idiom?"

"I think you've got it, buster," replied Bradley with a grin. "So, this is the famous TT-33. Where do you people make your ammo? Chernobyl?"

"Yes, and it glows in the dark. Go ahead, shoot it."

After blasting away with the piece, Bradley could not refrain from laughing. "Man, is that for real? Good grief, that's a lot of slide travel."

"It has to be, it's a long machine gun cartridge. It's a bottleneck, very powerful, five hundred foot-pounds at the muzzle. Even more sometimes. This Sellier ammunition is *so* powerful."

"Well, I'll tell you, Osipov," Bradley quipped, returning the weapon, "you can shoot through the car door with this thing, and if you miss, when they get out I'll knock 'em down with my 1911. It's the greatest knockdown round out there."

"You have a good imagination."

"Hey, sell the Kremlin."

The girls, as Gretchin loved to say, found their own camaraderie. Unimpressed with the ranch as a whole, they turned their attention to its kitchen. Keeping out of the cook's way, they baked pies and cakes and reminisced about their careers in teaching. Martina said she had to fatten up her starving Russian husband. Gretchin and Maggie seemed bent on learning each other's recipes. The heavyset cook said the women were too skinny to survive in Idaho and needed more meat on their bones.

At the range, they traded guns for fun and laughed at their attempts to hit the moving targets. The three had decided to carry their weapons in their purses, instead of holstered in some odd place under a coat, blouse, or skirt. They had learned in the small arms training that accessing your weapon was crucial, and now every day at the range they practiced scenarios of accessing from their purses and firing from various positions.

One evening in February, Gretchin, who had retreated to her room to write letters, opened her door to an oddly smiling Bradley.

"You know," he said, leaning into the doorway, "you could come to my room and we could talk or something."

"You're illiterate," she returned, twisting her lips. "How could we talk? What would we talk about?"

"Well, we could play cards or something."

She blinked. "Cards?"

"Yeah. Why not?"

"Cards? That's pathetic."

"You can't just sit alone in your room all the time."

Incredulous, she shook her head. "Excuse me?"

"You need to socialize, and you and I should work on getting along better, don't you think?"

"You're my psychologist, right?"

He stared at her.

"If not," she continued, "you're a presumptuous idiot, right?"

"Can't you just say it was a bad suggestion?"

Her tone was cold. "No."

His eyes traveled over her hair. "You're sure you don't want to come over?"

"Yes."

With a shrug, "I'm just trying to be friendly."

"No," she said, her hand still on the doorknob, "you're hitting on me. And your advances are not welcome. So, goodbye."

"You're just being nasty because you have to. You'd feel insecure if you couldn't be nasty."

Her tone even colder, "You're a jerk, and you're hitting on me. I'm not nasty because I have to be, I'm nasty because I want to be. It's intentional. It's my assessment that you, Mr. Hopkins, are the quintessential all-American jerk."

He reddened, then hissed at her, "You know, Gretchin, I wouldn't share my life with you for all the medals in the Air Force. The president could present me with the Medal of Freedom, and I still wouldn't do it."

"You wouldn't share your life with me—really? Okay."

"Oh, and for your information, I just wanted to talk."

"No," she retorted. "No, you absolutely did not. You wanted to screw me on impulse because we're stuck here together and you were bored. And now you feel really stupid about it, don't you, mister fucking prick Air Force?"

Momentarily, "I am not illiterate."

"You are."

"I'm not."

"You are."

He pointed at himself. "I've been to college. Think about it, I couldn't be illiterate."

"You're a moron," she said with finality, closing the door slowly until it clicked shut.

Raising his voice, he yelled through the closed door, "I am not a moron, Gretchin! Think about it, I could not be a moron, I'm the principal. You're just a teacher, I'm higher than you, Gretchin. I am not a moron."

Maggie, who had opened her door at the commotion, leaned out and said calmly, "We heard you, Bradley, we heard you."

His eyes large, he turned and walked back to his room.

"Why is it, Osipov," he queried the next day, during a short hike to the frozen stream, "that women wear low necklines to get you to look at them but then call you a dirty old man when you do? Is it the same in Russia?"

"My English is not very great," replied the other, "but I think *dirty old man* puts you in my generation. I would not use the term and drive a Corvette, as you do. How old are you?"

"Forty-two this year."

A theatrical shrug. "I will be sixty."

"I know. I saw your profile when we targeted you, remember?"

Ignoring him, Stanley said that of course it was the same in Russia, that it was all just part of the sex war between men and women.

"But you like women, obviously."

"Russian women are crazy. I can tell you this is the truth. American women are crazy, too."

"But Martina's German. What about the Germans? They're too organized to be crazy."

Stanley laughed. "No, they are worse."

"But we're not allowed anymore to say these things."

The Russian winked. "Yes, I understand. But the women are allowed to talk about us."

"Of course."

"Which demonstrates the wisdom of humanity. Humanity has no wisdom. It only has a market-place, a mall that feels good and smells sweet, where truth is a commodity. If a man thinks women are crazy, he is scorned for saying it. If a woman thinks men are crazy, she is applauded for saying it. At least, for now. It all depends on what is popular, what they are selling on TV and in the movies."

"Well," replied Bradley, "you shoot straight and your cowboy boots look great. So, viva rednecks."

Toward the end of the third week in February the weather changed dramatically. The sun shone very bright, the daily temperatures rose to above freezing. Everyone sensed that something was forthcoming from Kessler. Upon a very sunny day, at lunchtime, he called Martina and said the team should get ready to go and that he was sending the plane the next day to get them. The current project was still on and the team would be briefed on the plane.

No one slept more than a few hours that night.

Stanley cleaned and readied both weapons and checked the ride of the Makarov, which he carried simply stuck into the waistband of his jeans. The TT, its nose too long and heavy for waistband carry without a holster, he would carry holstered, small of the back. Satisfied, he retrieved the photo bag, cleared the D80's SD card, set the dial to Programmed Auto, and cleaned the two zooms he had brought. Considering the pro D3 too heavy, he had left it in Vermont.

"You must clean your gun," he reminded Martina, watching her undress.

"I know that, sir," she said playfully, "you don't have to tell me."

"How does it feel to be team leader? Will it make you cold again?"

"Cold?"

"Yes, like a spy."

"Yes," she mused, "I guess we are spies now, aren't we?" She shook her head. "I don't know. Don't let me become cold, Stanley, okay?"

"Well, come to bed, and we will be hot spies."

"No," she replied, a sparkle in her eyes, "I have to clean my gun. It has to be clean, because I sleep with it, remember?"

In the morning, the sun sent razors of light through the trees, as if it meant to promise an early spring. The few cloud puffs floating in the brilliant blue sky were blown away before noon. Small animals came out of the surrounding forest to play at the edges of the compound, only to flee again when the snowplow's burners ignited and the truck began its slow journey up and down the runway. There was no snow to clear, but all the ice would have to be gone before the Otter could land. In the middle of the afternoon, just above the tree line, the plane appeared.

"Normally," said Maggie to no one in particular as the team watched the Otter's wheels touch down, "I would take a beta-blocker even for an airliner. And here, I expect to be briefed on a roller coaster."

Martina pushed her sunglasses on. "Take one, Maggie. It'll be fine. Did you see that? Unless I'm wrong, the Connors woman is on the plane."

In less than an hour, the plane was refueled and the luggage packed on the seats to distribute weight. Kelly Connors and the pilot were drinking coffee beside the Otter's open door when the team began to climb in and take their seats.

With everyone in, Connors climbed in and pulled the door and secured it. The pilot started the Pratt & Whitney's, gave them a minute to heat up, then taxied across to the end of the runway. After turning the plane carefully, the pilot lined up, throttled up, released the brakes, and blew down the tarmac.

The strong lift of the Otter's long wingspan brought them up quickly. Maggie closed her eyes as they left the ground. Bradley held two fists aloft. When they had reached cruise altitude, Connors unbuckled and turned around. As she was about to speak she caught Bradley's broad grin.

"Yeah?" she queried impatiently.

"This is a three hundred, isn't it?" he asked. "I looked it up after we came in." When she only stared at him, as if at a monkey in a zoo, he continued, "It's a DHC-6 Series 300 with Pratt & Whitney PT6A-27's cutting the air. That's an amazing engine. Turboprop." Still she stared. "I mean, it's not a big GE or a rocket. This is a utility plane, very serviceable."

She made no response, but merely pushed the hood of her parka back and then shook her hair loose. He stared open mouthed, for he found the pale eyes framed by the shaken-out hair mesmerizing. She had not impressed him before, trussed in her gray suit, standing like a sentry in the school room or serving coffee at the hotel briefing, and certainly not slouched in her parka, chatting with the pilot beside the plane before takeoff. But now, with her unearthly eyes, her face wreathed with the radiant hair, she touched in him a nerve that left him momentarily unable to speak further.

"All roight," she said to everyone, her accent thick as clover, "here's the briefin'. Paul couldn't come, so I'm here. I don't speak well, so speak up if yous don't understand me."

"Is there," queried Martina gently, "material, uh, written material?"

"No, et's joost me. Lat me know ef I'm not clear. Et's impartant yous understand me."

Although the heavy Irish combined with the drone of the engines seemed to her ridiculous, Martina replied, "We'll let you know, Kelly, yes."

Blinking, Connors proceeded to inform them that because of an anonymous tip the Agency believed the Russian woman implicated in the murders to be again in Philadelphia. Stanley should attempt to contact the woman again and confront her about the murdered couple. The team should draw up a plan of involvement and be ready for a serious altercation. They were all to assume their lifestyles as in the old advisory team, except as being retired, etc. Martina's and Maggie's old house in Lawncrest had been procured by the Agency. They could move in and refurnish at will. For the present, the team was to be based in or near Philadelphia. The present flight, she said, would connect them with a major airport, from which they were to take a commercial flight to Philadelphia.

"Our old house?" responded Maggie. "Really? Amazing."

The pale eyes seemed pleased. "It's a pairfect setup."

Bradley ran a hand along the top of his head. "I haven't sold my house yet, or my car either. So, I'm good."

Gretchin nodded in agreement. "My studio's right where I left it and my lease is great for now. Sounds good."

"We will have to get our things from the farm," Stanley put in.

Connors produced a smile. "We'll have that done for yous, don't worry about et. Actually I'm makin' the arrangements mesalf."

Martina, obviously uneasy, asked, "By serious altercation you mean a fight, I suppose." When there was no response, she continued, "And what do you want us to do if there is, defend ourselves?" Still there was no response. "The Agency has to give us some guidance here. It's only reasonable. You've given us little data to work with. You tell us to be creative and all that, but things could go absolutely awry, as I'm sure you can appreciate. What then? And what is our basic initial purpose? If you could be a little more specific, it would be helpful. And are there any documents about this woman?"

"Well," replied Connors momentarily, "et's pratty semple. Get all the information yous want to, but then don't lat 'am get away."

Maggie tipped her head. "Meaning? If this woman or these people try to escape, what do you want us to do?"

The answer was matter of fact. "Kell 'am."

There followed this statement a silence broken only by the drone of the engines.

Maggie raised her eyebrows and cleared her throat. "That's quite severe. Is that the official order?"

Now clearly annoyed, Connors wiped her nose with the back of her hand. "You're fuckin' roight."

Maggie blinked. "You don't have to get angry, uh, Kelly. I didn't mean to slight you. It's just that, well, what you're asking us to do is, well, severe."

"Of carse et's sevaere, loike. You're in a sevaere bezzness. T'ese people are kellin'—not that I give two shets on the table, but the Agency does, and I'm workin' for the Agency, joost as yous are. T'ese people are murderers, for fuck's sake, and messy ones, at that. They've left a lot of carpses. Now we're goin' to leave theirs. So, get as much information as yous want about her connactions, but don't lat t'is woman or anybody weth her out of the city. Chase 'am ef yous have to, but stop 'am. T'is is yours briefin', and et's offecial. So, joost fuckin' do et."

"What information, Kelly," queried Martina, swallowing nearly audibly, "are we to look for?"

Annoyed again, "Nothin', joost keep yours ears open. Ef yous hear anything from her, remamber et, that's all. Then, loike, kell 'er."

"And if she surrenders?"

Momentarily, "That won't be a problam yous'll have to worry about, troost me. . . . Listen, ef yous can't do et, call me, I'll be there en a jeffy. Joost put a lamp cord around her nack and hold 'er till I get there."

Gretchin unzipped her parka. "Could I ask you something, Kelly?"

With an icy look, "Yous don't have to ask ef yous can ask, joost ask."

Gretchin cleared her throat. "Where will you be in all this? I'm not quite clear about that."

"I'll be around, and so will Packard. Joost call me cell, ef yous need me." Then she added, "Who knows, I moight knock on one of yours doors and ask for denner and a place to slape." Then, looking at Bradley, she added, "Maybe not yours."

He did not reply, but simply sat staring at her. Even as a shudder of turbulence suddenly went through the plane, lifting it and then dropping it, he continued to stare at her.

Again she wiped her nose. Then turning her attention to the Russian, she queried in a tone that sent a chill down Martina's neck, "And why're you so quoiet?"

He shrugged. "I have nothing to say, except that I am not an assassin."

"Aye," she said mockingly, with a glance at Martina. "And now you're a hoosband."

"That is correct. But I said I would help, and I will try it the best to help."

"*Do my best*," Martina corrected gently.

"Yes," he said, "I will do my best. But I am not an assassin. I am a photographer, not a killer."

A faintly macabre grin. "You mean, loike me."

"I did not say that," he replied. "But like I said to everyone, it does not exactly seem like you are translator."

"No," she returned. "Oi don't speak well."

CHAPTER 9

Philadelphia, March

As Connors had said, the house in Lawncrest was waiting. When Maggie had sold it upon retiring, she had not wished to deal with the furniture, however nostalgic, and had let it go to the new owner. Now the house was barren, except for three cots and a new refrigerator.

"Can I say *spooky*?" Maggie said, stepping into the living room.

"I suppose," Martina replied. "It's slang, but just say it."

"How many times have I walked through this door?"

"Good Lord, Maggie, do we want to conjure these memories? I never thought I would see this house again."

The Russian stood quiet as they talked. He too was remembering.

Martina touched his arm. "Well, Mr. Osipov, are we ready to make this our home?"

"I think that decision has already been made by the Agency."

"Yes," she agree. "We'll need to get the place furnished in quick order."

It was on a Saturday evening, three weeks later, that Bradley wheeled the Corvette to the curb, got out, trudged around to the passenger side, opened the door, and then waited impatiently for Gretchin to swing her legs out. "Never thought I'd see this place again," he offered, shutting the door with his fingertips.

She responded derisively, "We're late, thank you."

Although initially he had been annoyed at having to give her a ride, he was determined not to let her get to him this evening.

She pressed her lips together, scanning the house. "I agree with Connors, it's perfect."

At the top step he pushed the doorbell. "Why don't you cut the trash talk tonight," he said, not looking at her, "we should just try to get along."

"With you?"

Then Maggie opened the door and let them in.

"God, it's beautiful," said Gretchin. "You did all this in three weeks?"

Martina gave her a smile for this, then took their coats.

"Is that," Gretchin queried, "your old couch?"

"No, but we've tried to match just about everything with the way it was. And since the movers brought our things from the farm, we're nearly back to where we were."

"So," observed Bradley, who had taken a seat upon one of the stuffed chairs, "this house is to be our base."

"Objections?" queried Martina.

He shook his head.

When coffee and tea had been passed, Martina, smiling perfunctorily, said, "Well, we should get down to it, then. Stanley has made contact with the woman, and she will see him. He's to go there tomorrow night. I called Connors and gave her the address where they're to meet. It's a house in the northeast again."

"God, that was fast," said Gretchin. "How did you reach her, Stanley?"

He scratched his head. "I simply called my contact's old number, and she answered, just like before."

"The woman we're after answered?"

"No, my contact. And when I told her I wanted to talk to the woman who dismissed me, she said okay and gave me a phone number. It was so quick, it was amazing to me. I did not argue."

Gretchin chuckled, "I would think not."

Surreptitiously Bradley watched her as she took a cookie and then drew a leg up under herself. She had stolen a glance in his direction. Carefully he sipped the hot coffee, fighting an urge to look at her sweater. The cleavage she sported had always worked its magic on him. His eyes had gone there so many times, but not anymore. Heck no. He looked at Martina's sweater, then at Maggie's, and tried to imagine the differences in their breasts. And why shouldn't he? He could look at anybody's breasts, he determined, anybody's he wanted to. But he would not look at Gretchin's, not anymore.

"Hey," she said, throwing a twinkling glance in the direction of everyone except Bradley, "this is just like old times, isn't it? Even the same teapot."

Maggie, pleased, replied, "Oh, yes. I'll never get rid of that. It's more than an heirloom, it's part of who we are."

The next evening, at eight o'clock, Stanley shut down the rental car's engine, put the keys into his jacket pocket, and got out. Careful to avoid glancing toward Martina and Maggie, parked across the street, or toward Bradley's Corvette, parked a few spaces behind him, he zipped his jacket halfway down and walked up the pavement to the front door. It was at moments like this that he wished he could be more Zen, more in control of his nerves. He drew his breath and pushed the buzzer. Momentarily the door cracked open, and he saw the same eyes, the same mouth, the same wretched face as before. And again, cigarette smoke wafted from the open door.

"Yes, come into the house," she said. "I will take your coat," she offered as she closed the inside door. She was forced to fiddle with the deadbolt to get it to go home.

Unzipping the jacket completely, he replied, "I will keep it on, thanks."

She eyed him for this, but walked past him and led him, as before, into the living room. Glancing around, he could see that it was all as shabby as the other house had been. Certainly it reeked even more of smoke. He waited for her to sit, then took the chair facing her.

"It is a good thing to see you again," she said at length, her little eyes glimmering.

"Yes," he replied. He watched as the mouth of the fat, makeup-caked face cracked into a a smile.

"I do not remember exactly," she said, "what I told you before this time, but I am remembering, it is possible, that I told you not to ever come back. Do you remember that? Is it that I am correct?"

He waited for the smile to fade, then replied, "I remember. You are correct."

Again the awful smile, then a slow, deliberate, "What do you want?"

He looked into the eyes and wondered, for they twinkled at him, where exactly this part of humanity got the audacity to attempt to smile and be charming. "I am noticing," he said, "that there is no carpet."

She glanced down. "Yes. It is a different house. They do not have a carpet here. They are cheap."

"Maybe it is because of the economy."

"Yes, ha."

"Actually," he said, "I wanted to ask you about the people in the other house. They were murdered." He watched as her expression did not change.

"That is terrible."

"No," he returned, "that is not what I am meaning. Why did you have them killed?"

Any charm she had been effecting now disappeared, as if up some magician's sleeve, leaving only an ominous sobriety. "I am not alone at this house."

He sighed, "Really?"

"I did not have them killed," she said smugly, "I did the killing of them myself."

"Why?"

"So, you go and marry the CIA spy, the German woman, and then you are coming here and you ask me about killing people. You are stupid." She shrugged. "Sometimes I kill people just for the reason that I am not trusting them."

"You killed them because you did not trust them?"

"And," she said, raising her hand and pointing at him with a yellowed forefinger, "I do not trust *you*."

"You should know," he said slowly, deliberately, "that you are giving Russia and all Russians a bad name, a bad image."

"And you are not doing this, by marriage to the German—*awk!*—and going over to the Americans? I see your cowboy boots there. But German woman—*German*—she is the shit!"

"Marrying a German," he replied, "is part of being an American. It is democratic."

She produced a yellow, malicious grin. "You are defending America?"

He shook his head no.

"You are the shit," she continued, spitting her words, "and the German is the shit!"

"You are saying bad things about my German wife, and you are saying bad things about me. You do not like Russians to marry Germans. But you come to America and drive the Chevrolet."

"Yes," she laughed, her eyes going shut with delight, her hands moving as if manipulating a steering wheel, "I still have Chevy. I drive it everywhere, and I listen to radio."

"And you kill people because you do not trust them."

"Yes," she said, becoming serious. And giving him a nod, she said again, "And I do not trust *you*."

"You are making Russia look bad. You are a bad advertisement, you are not good for business."

She raised her hand and pointed at him again. "You are defending America."

"No," he replied, "I am defending Russia."

He waited until she lowered the hand, then slid his own hand along his belt, closed his fingers around the grip of the Makarov, and slipped it out. He had left it chambered and cocked, safety off. Time did not seem to be passing. Her little eyes bulging, she clenched her yellow teeth at him as he brought the gun to level. He did not wish to say anything more to her. Deftly he aimed at the center of her chest and pulled the trigger twice—*Blat! Blat!* She yelled wretchedly, clutched her sweater, and lay writhing in the chair. He stood as she writhed and quickly stepped beside her chair, put the muzzle to her rolling head, and fired twice—*Blat! Blat!*

For only a moment he looked at the still head, then turned and took the hallway to the kitchen. His phone rang, and it was Martina.

"We heard the shots," she said frantically, "are you all right?"

"Yes," he answered, holding the pistol nearly straight out in front of him.

"We're at the front door."

"I am in the kitchen," he reported.

"Stay there! Connors is with us. Stay there!"

And then he heard the blast and looked down the hallway. Connors was in first, a short pump in her hands.

"Osipov!" she barked.

"I am here," he replied, leaving the kitchen, the Makarov down. "She said she was not alone. What do you want to do?"

"Chack the house, all of et. There's a cellar?"

"Probably. It is typical," he said, reaching into his jacket for the LED.

The others were in now, and he watched as Martina's face became grim at the sight of the woman's bloody head.

Bradley puffed his cheeks, then exclaimed, "Whoa, is she dead, Osipov?"

"I cannot imagine that she is alive," he replied. "Impossible." He noticed that they all had their guns out, and he thought for just an instant that it was an odd thing, for they had been advisors, not agents. But Connors was halfway up the stairs now, so he turned and followed her.

At the landing, she called down to Martina, "Stand at the cellar door. Don't go down."

Then, with no hesitation, she strode boldly into the first bedroom, the shotgun aloft. Behind her, he flipped up the light switch. Room by room, they checked the entire house, but found nothing to indicate anyone else had been there.

"Nobody alse is here," she said with finality when they had gathered again around the dead woman.

They waited for her to make the next move or just to say something. She said nothing, however, but simply stepped over the gory chair, put the shotgun's muzzle to the woman's cheekbone and fired—*Boom!*

"Good gracious!" Bradley nearly yelled, recoiling as the woman's face was blown into a spray of blood and flesh.

Gretchin, her whole body cringing from the blast, simply exclaimed, "My God!"

But turning back to them, Connors merely pulled the pump, slammed the next shell home, and said, "Dedn't want her to get away." And striding past them to the front door, she said, "All roight, lat's get the fuck out."

At the door, she stood aside until they were all out. As the Russian passed by pushing the Makarov back into his waistband she said, "Guass you dedn't naed the lamp cord."

"No," he replied, looking for a moment into the colorless eyes. "And I did not call you."

"No, but your woife ded. Guass she dedn't want to lose you."

And when he turned away from her and walked through the door she followed him. She did not bother to turn out the lights or to close what was left of the door.

During the night, Martina awoke from a troubled sleep and reached out for him. Feeling only cold sheets, she knew that he had been unable to sleep himself and had probably gone down to the kitchen for a bowl of cereal. But as she lay there she reminded herself that during the drive home he had not seemed anxious at the killing. She had only known him as a photographer, an artist, not someone like this, and if she had been asked beforehand whether she considered him capable of doing such a thing, she would have answered no and said that she only knew him to be a sensitive man. And yet now she could not but see the woman's head after he had shot her to death.

Slipping into her robe, she went down to the kitchen. He was sipping a cup of herb tea. He did not seem troubled.

"Can't sleep?" she asked softly, opening a cupboard for a cup.

"No," he replied, "I cannot sleep. And now I think you are going to ask me how exactly I could have become a killer."

"It was on my mind, I confess."

"I did carry a gun sometimes with the KGB. They made me do it, but I wanted to do it, anyway. I never shot anyone with it, but I did enjoy having it and carrying it. It reminded me of my father, and it seemed with the gun I had become more a part of his life. But I did like carrying the gun for myself too. It was a Makarov, a beautiful gun, just like this one. I practiced with it a lot. And I saw them kill people—people they said were criminals, but still, people, humans, actual living creatures. I suppose, that experience led to this. I do not know. But I knew, after talking to the woman, that I must shoot her. It was very simple. And I am sorry that it was very simple. Please forgive me to know that I would do it again. It was not a mistake."

"I'm actually sorry," she whispered, "that you had to do it. I know those were the instructions, but doing it must be a completely different animal."

"I have heard this expression—*different animal.* It is strange for you to say it. It makes me think of the bear the KGB shot in the face."

When the kettle whistled she filled the cup, selected a tea, and took a seat beside him.

"Like I told you," he continued gloomily, "the killing of the bear broke my heart into pieces. It changed me totally forever. I know that the nightmares I have about it will never stop. But this project did not break my heart. But it is still true that I have killed a human being. This woman, no matter how bad a killer she was, did not make the request to come into the world."

"You are showing sympathy," she said, her tone matter of fact.

"Since she was a person, yes," he protested. "She was a person, a *person.*"

"A person who murdered other persons."

"But still a person. A living mind and body."

Softly she replied, "That is not our concern, I think. At least, it isn't mine. Someone once said to me, 'just kill them and let God sort it all out'."

He shrugged helplessly. "That is harsh."

"So was this woman's treatment of her victims."

"Yes, I know this completely. I am only saying that it is not the easy thing to kill a human being."

"Again," she persisted, "that isn't our concern. I will leave that with anthropology and the church. My concern is that she was a criminal, a very evil and dangerous one. If you had not killed her, she would no doubt have killed, *murdered* many others. The victims, Stanley, were also human beings. Our concern is that she was a dangerous person, if you will. She made her own choices in life. We all do. We take the paths we do by the choices we make."

He gave a simple nod. "Yes, I am completely understanding this."

She sighed. "Good."

"But," he said, pushing his cup away, "I am certain, since I have made this choice and accepted this path, that there will be others."

"Yes," she said softly, "I agree. I have never shot anyone, let alone killed anyone. If the Agency is going to use us in such a capacity, I have to prepare myself for it. And practicing with the gun won't really help, I think."

"No," he replied, "it will not help."

She looked at him and let her eyes follow the lines in his face. "I love you," she said.

"Connors said you called her to come, because you didn't want to lose me."

"Yes."

He put his hand on hers. "I need your love to me. And I am having only love for you."

Then she leaned close and kissed his lips softly. "Come back to bed," she whispered. "Let's try to sleep a little more. Even if we can't sleep, just closing our eyes and resting will be essential, I should think."

He smiled. "You are talking like the team leader and not the wife."

She too smiled. "Forgive me."

It was just before five that Connors rang at the door. Wearing a leather bomber jacket, she strode in and took a seat on the couch.

"Tea?" queried Maggie.

"Aye, t'anks."

"It'll be just a minute."

When Stanley and Martina sat down, Connors asked, "How're you holdin' oop, loike, Osipov?"

"I am thinking I will live."

"Well," she continued, "et had to be done. T'anks for not lattin' her get away. She dedn't even make et out of her chair."

His brow furrowed at this attempt at levity. Somehow, he could not imagine her making jokes. "But," he said, "you think there are others?"

She nodded. "Yeah, and we're goin' to get 'am. They're still around, loike, we're pratty certain. They were en the house, prob'ly, and left when they heard your shots. I'd have left, mesalf, loike." She grinned, looking at him, then at Martina. Then, her expression sober, she said, "You said you weren't an assassin, but that was an assassination, if I ever saw one. That's quite a gun you've got there, mester. You're not just a photographer, at least not anymore."

He watched gloomily as she grinned again.

"Well," she said, carefully taking the saucer and cup of steaming tea from Maggie, "we t'ink we know where they are. Packard followed a suspecious-lookin' car last noight droivin' away fast from that neighborhood."

"So," put in Maggie, "Mr. Packard was there?"

"Carse he was, we both were. Don't t'ink we'd lat yous go en naked, loike, do yous? How do you t'ink I got there so fast? . . . But ef the ones en the car came out of the house, he says they drove to a single house not far away. We're goin' en tonoight, and we'll need ever'body there." She paused to take a sip of the tea. "Aye, t'at's fuckin' good, loike, t'anks."

"We're all going?" quered Maggie.

"Yeah, but this toime, I'm goin' en first."

Martina, watching her sip the tea, wondered how in the world such a beautiful woman ever got into such a line of work. But then, she herself had been called beautiful, as had Maggie, and yet here they were in that same line of work. There was no need to remind herself that beauty had nothing to do with it. Perhaps genetics did or just the overall spin of nature. Even the woman they had shot last night had perhaps been beautiful at one time, and yet there she was, a villain so evil she needed to be dispatched not merely efficiently but in such a gruesome manner.

"All roight," said Connors, setting the cup down. "The plan's pratty semple. When we get there, ever'body stays en the cars. I'll go up to the door and talk me way en. Ef they try to get out the back, Packard'll kell 'em. We can't lat 'am escape. One chance, t'at's et. Get your stuff togather. I called the others. We're meetin' 'am there in an hour."

CHAPTER 10

It was indeed a mere hour later that Stanley pulled to the curb and parked in front of Connors' gray car. She was on the phone as they passed and didn't seem interested in being interrupted. He shut the engine off and looked at Martina, then in the mirror at Maggie.

Martina gave a subtle wave through the windshield to Gretchin and Bradley, parked across the street. She heard Connors' door being shut as Stanley lowered his window. Then the eerie eyes peered in at them.

"Don't come en," she said in a low voice, "unless I call yous. Packard's out back now. But be ready. E f they come out, loike, just follow their car, et's that one over there, then call Packard. I'll prob'ly be dead, ef they come out."

Then she simply turned and walked away, zipping up the jacket, her hands bare. As she climbed the front steps, she pulled a band loose to let her hair fall, then pushed the doorbell. In a moment, the inside door was opened by a woman and the storm door pushed open just a little.

"Okay," said Stanley softly, "she is going in."

They watched as the inside door was closed, then waited. One minute passed. Then they heard shots—*Pop!—Pop!—Pop!—Pop!—Pop!*

"Good Lord," breathed Maggie.

"Wait," said Martina, clutching her phone.

Then five more shots sounded, a pause, then sporadically five more. Then a single booming shot clearly from outside the house.

As Martina held her breath Connors suddenly emerged from the house, then calmly descended the steps. They waited as her unhurried pace brought her nearer.

"Droive," she commanded Stanley as she passed the window.

Immediately he started the engine, but waited until she was inside her car and had shut the door. Then he pulled away from the curb just as the Corvette passed them from the opposite direction. He drove slowly, checking the mirror as Connors' car followed. At the corner, he turned left, but she turned right, and he watched the mirror again briefly as her car disappeared into traffic.

When Martina's phone rang, she threw the slider up with force. "Kelly?" she answered. . . . "Now? Are you okay? . . . Are you sure? We can meet you there. . . . You're sure? . . . Okay, okay. Let us know, if you can. . . . Right, got it." Closing her eyes as she closed the phone, she announced, "Uhm, she's been shot and is driving herself to the hospital. She said it wasn't bad and we were just to go home."

In just under an hour Connors showed up at the house, sporting only a slight limp as she climbed the front steps. Not waiting to be shown to a seat, she strode to the couch and ripped open the flaps of a nylon satchel. Gingerly she spread out four fresh eight-by-ten color prints even as Maggie reached to get her a cup of tea.

"Careful," Connors winced, protectively snatching up the photos, "people would kell for these."

Bradley retrieved a cookie, then sat back and put his leg up. "What happened at the house? What'd you do in there?"

Sitting back herself, she sighed. "Lat's joost say, they won't be doin' no more shoppin', those people. Looks loike they were accomplices. I got the woman and a man. Packard got a guy goin' for the kitchen dar. They looked Russian or some such. Kassler's got the specs on tham. We t'ink that's all there was though, we t'ink we've fennished et."

Maggie, closing her mouth, sat staring, but then queried, "So, uh, they're dead?"

"Moight say."

Gretchin blew air from her puffed cheeks and pushed a wad of hair behind an ear. "You know, um, this is getting pretty serious."

"What'd you expact, a fuckin' Disney movie?"

"No," was the quick reply, "but maybe a raid or something, and maybe an arrest, something like that. I mean, that's reasonable. But this is—"

Connors blew across her tea, glancing around at them. "Look," she said after taking a sip of the tea, "et shouldn't have to be explained to yous. These people were murderers. Whatever they were into, they were lavin' a trail of fuckin' carpses, loike. They had to be stopped. And there's others that have to be stopped, too, and the Agency can't set down weth each of yous and explain why they have to be stopped. We'd been trackin' these people, and there was no way to breng 'am to joostice, there was no way. A lot of the people we deal weth are loike that. They're creminals, for fuck's sake, yous have to see that. They're shet."

Maggie trained an ear. "They're what?"

"I think," offered Martina politely, "she said they're shit."

"T'at's roight," Connors affirmed. "There's no other way to get people loike this. Interpol can't get 'am. Their own people can't get 'am. They fly way under the radar, and they know how to stay there. They're so far beyond the constables, what would yous suggest, givin' 'am a fuckin' parkin' ticket?"

Bradley snickered at this, then gave his nose a swipe.

Gretchin, sobered, replied softly, "No. I only thought I was in for something a little more civilized."

"Civilized? Jesus wept, you can't be sarious. What're you t'inkin' about, their roights or some such?"

"Well, no—"

"I should t'ink not. Look, we can't set down with each of yous and hold your fuckin' hand. They're kellin' people."

"So are we," was the weak reply.

"T'at's defferent, loike," Connors shot back. "We're not kellin' people joost for fun. Nothin' wrong weth that, of course, but we're kellin' people to save people, and ever' one of yous can see that. Look, we need yous to work for us. Et's a good team, all of yous. But yous're workin' for the Agency, and ef the Agency says to put somebody down, they need to be put down, loike. Et's as semple as that, and if yous can't see et, yous better speak oop now. But ef yous're en, you're en, and you'll, loike, pull the trigger when we say to."

"You know, Kelly," replied Martina at length, "I think we've got that. I think it would be good," and here she glanced at the others, "if we took a little vote of affirmation maybe. We have all thought these things through pretty much already, I'm sure. How about it, everyone, vote of affirmation? Or if not, as Kelly just said, please speak up now."

Bradley, playing with his shoestring, responded immediately, "I'm in, I'm okay with everything. That's exactly what criminals do, anyone can see that. They operate totally beyond the civil authorities."

Martina nodded. "Obviously, and they have to be stopped by people like us, who also operate beyond the civil authorities. It's an unpleasant job, but it must be done."

"Yes," chimed Maggie. "Yes, I agree."

Connors looked at Gretchin. "How about you?"

Slowly Gretchin drew a breath, then let it out. "Yes, I agree, too. I understand and of course I've already thought it through. . . . But God, that was brutal."

Connors' lip curled as she addressed Stanley. "We should ask the Russian. You're the only one of yous that's shot anybody yet. How about you?"

"You keep using *Russian* as a negative term," he said slowly.

Martina put in, "A *pejorative*."

Connors gave him a gritty look. "Do I?"

"Well," he sighed, "it is like I said before. I am not an assassin, miss County Cork," here he gave her a simple smile, "but I am agreeing with the others, and yes, I am finding everything to be acceptable."

She grinned at him, then said, "All roight, lat's get to work." And leaning forward, she dropped the prints onto the coffee table. "Look at these pictures. They're, loike, the next people we have to see."

CHAPTER 11

Jacksonville, Florida, June

St. Johns Avenue seemed dreamy to Martina as she piloted the gray SUV through the bluish Florida night. Stanley, still asleep, his head buried in a pillow against his window, had not responded at her announcement that they were almost there. Even Maggie, stretched out in the back seat, had given no reply.

"I don't understand," Martina muttered, "why you people are so lethargic. We've only driven a thousand miles."

"Oh, dear," responded Maggie, "what did you say? Are we there?"

"No, not quite yet, it'll be a few more minutes. Go back to sleep."

Maggie sat upright and blinked. "Did you find anything on the radio?"

"No, just country and a few rock stations. There's one here in Jacksonville that the search has been picking up since we left Georgia and even before, called the Big Ape, or some such, pop-rock, I think. It's hilarious, but only that."

"Sorry, dear."

"Well, I don't mind country music anymore, as you know, due to someone we all love and won't mention, asleep here in the front seat with his cowboy boots on. In fact, I think I've learned to like it a little. It's not Wagner or Strauss, but it keeps you awake at the wheel."

"And the pop-rock?"

A groan. "Oh, Maggie, that stuff is tedious. But we are in Jacksonville. We have been driving under moss hanging from the trees, and it is a lovely summer night, very warm out, but nice."

"Well, why not roll the windows down?"

"It seemed a little *too* warm for that, at least it did at the last rest stop. And there are a lot of bugs in the air, they're all over the windshield. I turned the wipers on, but it just smeared them."

"So, you've followed the map all right?"

"Directions were pretty clear."

"Why no GPS, I wonder? It's been that way all along."

Martina groaned again. "Yes. I don't know. It's been no computers, no internet, no GPS, and only regular cell phones, all since training."

"Even Kelly never uses the web, never talks about it. My goodness, look at the palm trees here. Some are quite short and thick."

"It's a little over the top, isn't it, how Paul doesn't want us to use a computer for anything concerning the team or a project. Sure it goes along with his theory, I get that, but it's still over the top. What'd he say, email's okay as long as it's just personal, and so's the internet for shopping and doing personal research, yet there's to be no internet use at all as to the projects?"

"It's his theory, dear, we didn't have to say yes. Personally I'm just going to try to enjoy Florida."

"I did roll my window down once. You would not believe the fragrance, orange blossoms, I should think. I would love to have them in my garden. Yes, Kelly's quite a girl."

"What kind of rifle are we carrying for her?"

"An M44 carbine, or something. It's Russian surplus, very powerful. The ammunition is in a can, like a large sardine can."

"Does it have a scope?"

"No, and it's right from the armory, wherever that is. It does have a rather wicked-looking bayonet that folds along it's side. It's a beautiful gun really, with blond wood—blond like her. I think Stanley admires her. But you've noticed, no tech stuff. I mean, she uses a Blackberry."

"That's for security—they can wipe it remotely, if it's lost or taken."

"I didn't know that. She's quite a girl."

"Woman, dear."

"Yes, right, *woman*. A beautiful woman with guts and a gun."

"And a brassiere."

"Uh-huh."

Stanley stirred, then raised his head sleepily. "What? Did I hear my name mentioned?"

"No," replied Martina dryly, "only the word *brassiere*."

"Whose?"

"Kelly's. We were talking about it, and I had mentioned that you admired her."

He sniffed and sat up. "I confess that you are correct."

"Why did your accent seem stronger when you said that, Stanley?"

He gave her a weary look. "I do not know the answer to this. Because it is typical of Russians maybe. What time is it?"

"It is almost two o'clock in the morning," she replied, returning the look, "and yes, if you're going to ask it, we are almost there."

"This is good," he said, closing his eyes for a moment. "This is very good. It has been a long trip. You have done so much driving. Thank you."

"I don't mind, it keeps my bottom from going to sleep."

"I will have to rub it."

Maggie cleared her throat. "I'm here in the room, and I didn't need to hear that."

It was not until that evening, after everyone had rested from the drive, that Martina tried to relax. But even as she took her iced orange juice and sat across from Maggie on the screened porch she felt her back begin to tighten. The lazy summer yard sounds that filtered in through the screens might normally have been sufficiently pastoral to ease such tension, but were not this evening.

"Did you sleep well?" asked Maggie.

"No. I don't think the nap was enough."

"Actually, I can see that, dear. My question was rhetorical. You need to get some night sleep, not day sleep, I think. Why not go back to bed, sleep through the night, and you'll be all set?"

"I can't stop mulling over the details of the project. I guess they're always going to be weird, right?"

"Sounds logical, dear. I'd get used to it."

"That's what Stanley says."

"What is that wonderful fragrance from the yard?"

"Seems like a combination of orange blossom and something else, cinnamon maybe."

"It's actually nicer here than in Bermuda. I can't believe it, and I think we're inside the city limits too. Connors said it was *in* Jacksonville. It's just so beautiful. I wouldn't mind retiring here."

"See if there's a cemetery close by."

"Very funny, dear."

With a shrug, as if to mimic her husband, "One retires from teaching. We did that. I'm not sure one retires from this."

"Perhaps not. So, we're in Woodmere? It's just lovely here. Gracious, the bugs make a noise, don't they?"

"Maggie, do you think we're under surveillance?"

"By whom, the Agency?"

A nod.

"Yes, I do, dear. They watch whomever they wish. Personally, I don't care if they do watch me, and maybe it's better if they do. What are they going to see, Ms. Margaret Swift-Jones taking a shower or sitting on the toilet? They're putting us in the Devil's way, dear, and somebody's got to keep an eye on us."

"Yes, if only to watch us die."

Maggie took a deep breath to savor the floral fragrances. "Well," she said at length, "if they watch me die, they can just bury me here. So, a cemetery isn't out of order, I suppose.

Early the next afternoon, Gretchin and Bradley, along with Connors and Packard, arrived in a commercially rented minivan. They had been directed to come in by commercial air, live in the same house with the others, and then leave, when directed, by car.

Bradley, proudly at the wheel, pulled them up behind the gray SUV, shut the engine down, and sat for a moment, as if with satisfaction. Then perfunctorily he checked the rearview mirror. "Everything's cool," he announced confidently.

Gretchin grimaced. "*Cool?*"

"Yes," he replied with a groan. "Nobody was following us, that's cool, right? Is that okay with you, Gretchin?"

"You've just driven us from the goddamn airport, that's all, and now you're checking things out and informing us that everything's cool?"

His hand tightened on the wheel. "Lay off, Gretchin. I mean it, just lay off, okay?"

"No," she retorted. "No, it's not okay. You're implying that I'm picking on you." And lowering her chin and giving him a look, "Which is stupid."

Not wishing to endure more of this fray, Connors and Packard both slid their doors back and climbed out.

"Thanks, Hopkins," said Packard, "great ride. Hit the back, would you? I wanna grab my luggage."

Bradley pushed the tailgate button. "Sure thing, Len."

"Oh, God!" laughed Gretchin. "Now it's *Len*, not *Mr. Packard*, huh?"

Pulling his door latch, he turned to her. "You know, you're a real moron sometimes. You know that, right? You've got that, right?"

Giving him the finger, she shot back, "Your IQ is lower than a walnut's, so just get over yourself, asshole."

Connors, frequently in contact with Kessler, said the team should prepare for a stay of at least a month. She also announced that the Agency was sending someone to prepare meals and take care of the housekeeping. Although Martina and Maggie had found the kitchen fully stocked, they decided to add their own touches to bring it more in line with their tastes. The plastic-topped coffee maker was put away. The microwave was at first unplugged, then ignored, then put away with the coffee maker. Both the refrigerator and pantry were refreshed from the local supermarket. Stanley and Bradley, following a long walk, reported that the neighborhood was fairly wealthy although not opulent. Gretchin, loathing the humidity, took two showers a day and spent the rest of the time watching the widescreen TV in the living room. Packard entertained himself with cleaning his two magnums while watching baseball on the little black-and-white set in his room.

Connors never relaxed. She kept to herself, spending most days alone in her room or on the back porch drinking whiskey or tea. From childhood her life had been solitary, and she knew in the deepest part of her that it would always be so. At times her sensitive side caused her to slide into a kind of loneliness dream, from which she believed she could only be awakened through sex or alcohol. Usually she chose the latter.

In Ireland she had learned weaponry from her father, a man of incorruptible commitment to the cause of the Republic. To that cause she and her mother lost him. So, it was not odd that now when she had nightmares they were often of his death. If he had been more a man of survival than of ideals, the nightmares might be dreams. But it was not to be so, for nature had marked him out for sacrifice. When he was dead and her mother had told her how much she thought her to be like him, she had turned away and spat. No, she was no idealist and was not about to lay her life upon any altar.

"I see you've settled in, Kelly," said Martina one day in passing her room. "Feel at home?"

The pale eyes looked up from the desk. "Not really," she replied, sighing as Martina took a step inside and leaned against the doorframe.

"And where's home for you?"

Defensively, "Where's yours?"

With an amiable shrug, "I guess, it's here right now."

"So's moine."

"Uh-huh, right. But if you could be anywhere else, where would you like to be?"

"Hadn't t'ought about et."

"Uh-huh. Well, where would you like to retire, if you could? Ireland?"

Letting her pen fall with a plop, Connors looked at her, then replied, "I'm too young to retire."

"Yes, but hypothetically, what would you say?"

"I guess I'd say Ireland, sure, loike."

"Do you have someone there?"

"D'you mean a lover? No, not really. I have me ma, that's all, joost me ma. I had a dog, but he was shot."

"I'm sorry. Has anyone else close to you been shot?"

"Me dad, me dog, an uncle, and, loike, a few keds I knew from school."

"I'm sorry, Kelly."

The Irish eyes did not flicker. "Don't be, et's joost less to remamber."

"And that's true, you don't find yourself remembering?"

With a sigh, "Aye, I do remamber," and lifting a little glass beside the paper, "but that's what this is for."

"Uh-huh. Well, I certainly remember a lot I wish I could forget. But I have a lot of good memories too."

Momentarily, "Would you say you're happy?"

"Happy with Stanley? Yes, I would. I'm almost seventy."

"I know how old y'are."

With a smile, "Uh, yes, I'm sure you do."

"You don't look et."

"But I will. And who knows how much time there'll be left for us."

"T'en why're yous spendin' et loike this?"

Closing her eyes, "I am not sure. Why are *you* spending it like this?"

A chuckle. "God and the fuckin' saints only know. I'm not a regular agent, you know."

"No, I didn't."

"I'm sort of here on a deal, joost for the team."

"The team?"

"Aye, sort of *ad hoc*."

Blinking, "You're not regular CIA, Kelly?"

Connors lifted her chin, then replied, "No, they prob'ly wouldn't have me. They don't accept ever'body. They use a lot of people, but they don't accept ever'body. I was joost part of a deal. Short term. I'm part of Kassler's protaction for the team. He wanted some heavy stuff to roide along so's the rest of yous could be narmal. Et's part of his plan, you know that. He says he's seen too many intentional efforts wasted. He says sometoimes, loike, agents with too much trainin' and not enough experience joost fuck et up. People gat kelled who shouldn't, and people gat away who shouldn't. He knows yous're dysfunctional, and he even wants et that way to make yous loike narmal people. Anyways, I'm here so's yous can be narmal."

"Sounds a little cold. I mean, for us."

"Aye, you mean loike an exparimant, sher."

"And you're here only as needed."

"Aye. Et's me guess that the whole team's temporary, *ad hoc*," and with a sinister grin, "and disposable."

Swallowing, Martina stood straight, then leaned against the other side of the doorframe, "They put us on a fast track, you know, no red tape."

"Aye, they t'rew the same shet at me. They prob'ly do et that way so's there won't be too much on file when they have to gat rid of people. Same's for all of us, even Packard, joost temporary, that's my guess."

"You sound like my husband. He says he's got a bad feeling about the whole thing, the team, everything."

"I t'ink he's roight."

"What else do you think?"

The colorless eyes dropped, then looked up. "I t'ink the only friends this team has are each other."

"And Paul? Do you see him as a friend?"

Picking up the glass, "Nay."

"Stanley said something about survival."

"Bast to keep et en moind, I'd say. Et makes sanse."

"It made sense when dealing with the KGB too, I understand."

"The CIA, KGB, FSB, FBI—same fuckin' animal."

"And you don't see that animal as friendly?"

With a shrug, "Not to people loike us, or to et's enemies. But every country has an intelligence agency of sarts, so they must need 'am."

"How about the IRA, what would you say there?"

"They wouldn't exist ef someone didn't nade 'am. Nature's loike that, et sends what's naded."

"Do you see them as the same animal, too, like the CIA, KGB, like you said?"

"Nay, different."

"How so?"

An Irish smile. "More passionate."

The smile and the words gave Martina the sense that she was being offered a rare look at Kelly Connors. But life was like that, replete with masks that could only be lowered by the individual wearers, usually only upon the condition of trust. As she looked into the colorless Irish eyes she knew she was looking into the eyes of a friend. Then she said, "Passionate?"

"Aye. Less organization, more passion, I'd be sayin'."

A nod. "Oh, kind of like with us."

"The team?"

"Uh-huh," with a nod. Then, "Thanks for being candid with me. You didn't have to be, and I appreciate it."

"Sher. I t'ink we'd batter be steckin' togather though, all of us, ef any of et's true."

"Let me ask you, what do you follow in life?"

"What d'you mean?"

"Like, an ideology."

"Oh, I've got a few t'ings I believe en."

"And you see those things as right?"

Picking up the glass again, "I don't, loike, give a shet ef they are."

"So, morality's separate from ideology."

"Yeah."

Martina lowered her gaze. "Well, I'm not sure of much in life myself."

"Don't feel bad. Nobody's sher of anyt'ing. I'm not sher why I'm settin' here when I could be drenkin' tea with me ma and watchin' the screen."

"How about marriage?"

A shrug. "I'm t'irty-foive. I guess I could. I t'ink I joost wanna go home and get another dog."

"No man in the wings, huh?"

"No. I don't loike men very much. Most men joost wanna either fuck me or kell me or both. I've sher kelled a lot of tham."

Standing away from the doorframe, Martina turned to go. "Good to talk," she offered, "thanks, Kelly."

Another smile. "Sart of, blond to blond."

Next afternoon the housekeeper arrived by taxi. Connors said she would get the door, and when she opened it she looked for a moment into the woman's yellow eyes. Then she led the way through the house and out to the patio, where Maggie and Martina were serving up a light lunch they had prepared.

The team, except for Packard, were seated around a circular glass-topped table. The woman's eyes went immediately to Packard, who sat apart with a beer, hunched over a paper plate full of shrimp salad. She took in his two rubber-butted magnums, the jackass rig strapped over his short-sleeved dress shirt. She caught his eye as he threw her a glance, noting his obvious reluctance to acknowledge her.

"All roight," said Connors, "t'is is Ms. Bobbie Lee Henry, and she's here to help us out weth t'ings. See ef yous loike her, and make sher to tell her where stuff is."

The woman, pretty but distinctly not glamorous, did not blink at the brash introduction, but simply smiled, stepped forward, and with a heavy Southern accent said, "Yeah, you can all jist call me Bobbie Lee, if you want, or jist Bobbie, or whatever. I'm here to git your dinner, git some cleanin' done, watch the house, and jist help out. So, y'all please let me know if there's anything I miss, okay? And before you ask, I'm from Tinnessee. And, Mr. Packard, don't worry, them Smiths you got hanging out there, they don't bother me a bit. Six-eighty-sixes, I'll bet. I don't have one, but I've shot one. How do you like havin' seven shots?"

He blinked, then growled, "Fourteen."

"That's right," she chuckled, "you've got two of 'em. Well, I sleep with a Combat Magnum and I carry a P-64 Polish Makarov in a discreet place you don't wanna know about. And jist to let y'all know, I can take care of myself, so don't worry about me or the house when you're gone. That's what I'm here for. The Agency hired me, and this is my first assignment. I know all y'all's names, and I'm pleased to meet y'all."

Her utterly unpretentious manner coupled with the pleasantly twanged accent instantly put everyone at ease. Even Packard offered a genuine smile, at least such as he was capable of, and stood up sheepishly.

As he did she queried, "What d'you carry in those bastards, sir?"

He swallowed his mouthful of salad, then grunted, "Spreaders in this one and full metal in this one."

Her natural brown eyebrows lifting, she grinned at him. "Sounds logical, sir. And I'll bet you've got 'em pumped up with Corbon or some such. Bet they hit like a goddamn horse. Excuse my French, everybody, I'm from the hill country and don't know any better."

At this he stepped forward, placed his plate on the table, and courteously addressed her, as if officially. "Welcome. We're glad to have you with us."

She presented her hand, and he shook it.

Then Bradley quipped, "That's the closest he comes to sentiment, Bobbie Lee."

Maggie chimed, looking at the long chestnut-colored hair, "I think it is, yes. Have a seat, Bobbie Lee."

Smoothing back the hair, she drew a folding chair to the table and sat between Maggie and Martina, cognizant that the ice had been broken and even melted.

"Where in Tennessee?" asked Gretchin, reaching for a plate. "Can I get you a little salad? Is shrimp salad okay?"

"That'd be good, real good, yeah. Um, Mimphis."

"Memphis is in the hill country?"

Bobbie Lee eyed the dragon tattoo. "Not really, but I consider all of Tinnessee to be hill country. I was born in the sticks, went to high school near Mimphis, and then did some police work in the city there. They ricomminded me, the police did."

CHAPTER 12

The next morning, Sunday, Martina arose early to the smell of pancakes. Bobbie Lee stood before a square griddle of the piping cakes. Strips of bacon sizzled in a skillet. Plates were stacked on the kitchen table.

"Hey," said Martina, pulling a chair out. "It smells good in here, wonderful. Is that for us?"

"Yep. Ready in a minute. Everybody gittin' up? Don't wanna disturb anybody. I'll jist git it ready. Maybe I'll turn some gospel music on, y'know?"

"Sure, that would be great. Do you go to church, Bobbie Lee?"

Turning a pancake, "Sometimes. You guys go anywhere?"

"Stanley likes the Presbyterians. We go there sometimes."

"Stiff, at least for me."

"Uh-huh."

"I've gone to church a few times in Mimphis. Went to a Pentecostal church, maybe twice.

They're nuts, they're absolutely crazy, but they seem to have a good time. Presbyterians, yeah, a little formal. Anybody else go? Maggie?"

"She grew up Church of England, but doesn't go anywhere now, except when she goes with us. Kelly goes sometimes. She's Catholic."

"I figured."

"She might be leaving in a few minutes, if she's going. I heard her getting dressed. She might miss your breakfast."

"Oh, that's okay. I'm jist makin' it if anybody wants it. Yeah, Killy's kind of all right. Severe, a little severe. Swears like a sailor, as I'm sure the whole world has noticed. Hell, I couldn't swear that much if I tried."

"Yes."

"Anybody else? I'm jist askin', 'course, to git a lay of the schedule."

"I don't think Gretchin goes. Bradley used to go to a Baptist church, but I don't know if he goes now or if he'll go down here."

Turning another cake. "Yeah, that sounds right. How about Packard?"

"Uh, I don't think so, he'll probably just stay around here and clean his guns."

"Ha, yeah, well, he and me are gonna have a lot to talk about. I like guns, too. Grew up with 'em."

"So, do you like working for the Agency?"

"Again, this is my first assignment. But it seems okay." She shrugged as she poured another cake's worth of batter. "I'll tell you what, if they were lookin' for nationalists, they pritty much asked the wrong person in me. But then, sometimes I say too much."

"You didn't strike me as a flag waver anyway. We like you."

"Yeah, I'm the independent type. I told that Kissler guy that, but he said that didn't bother him. In fact, he said, he was lookin' for someone exactly like me to work with your team."

"That sounds like Paul."

"You're the team leader, they said. You think I'm okay, huh?"

"Most of us here can read people pretty well. So, yeah, everything's positive so far. And I think my husband will like your pancakes. He might be out of the shower now. See you in a bit."

"Yeah."

"The problem with this area," said the Russian to Bradley as the meeting began, "is that it is too humid."

The other crossed his legs. "But that's the beauty of it, Osipov, it makes everything like a greenhouse. That's why it's called Florida. Go back to Siberia."

"No, no, it is fine. I am very glad we have the AC."

"No argument there."

Martina, who had called the meeting, then spoke. "Okay, we're into our second week here. I have some news about the project. Paul called me with an update. The Agency is connecting this project to the one just completed. Evidence and new data show that the Russian woman Stanley met with and then shot was involved with a ring of poachers operating out of Africa and shipping to China. The Agency is fairly certain the current suspects are key figures in the ring. Intel shows that the suspects are somewhere in or around Jacksonville and that they will attempt to purchase and then sell a shipment of pelts of an endangered species. The shipment, sent from Texas through the Gulf, is actually here now. The buyers this time are believed to be domestic. Apparently the ring operates globally. In this case the species is the wolf of the Northern Rockies. The Agency wants them stopped right here, as too much mayhem is in their wake. They want them stopped here, before, during, or after the transactions are made."

"This is very interesting," observed Stanley, rubbing his chin. "So, the woman was probably using the Russian infiltration program as a cover for these activities."

Giving him a nod, "It seems that way."

"This seems consistent. I did not know of any criminal activities carried out as part of the program."

"Well," put in Bradley, "*I* don't want the Russians here, not infiltrating our society, I mean—you know what I mean. It's spying at the social level, which is wrong. And I'm sure other bad stuff goes along with it."

"It did not with me or with anyone I knew of."

"Societal infiltration is wrong."

"This is not the issue. The Russians are doing it to the Americans, and the Americans are doing it to the Russians, everybody knows this. Do not pretend that you are not doing it. It is the reality, whether we like it or do not like it. Look it in the face of it."

Martina frowned. "You mean, *face it*."

"Yes," he said, annoyed at her correction. "Yes, Bradley, face it."

Looking at the ceiling, Bradley said, "I don't need to face it, Osipov. I don't want you people here like that."

"Then do not send your Americans to us like that."

Connors, clearly annoyed with this exchange, said, "Our job's the projact, semple as that. So, lat's get et done." And looking to Martina, "Ded Kassler say anyt'ing else?"

"He said the pelts are sitting in a truck just outside the Naval Air Station, not far from here."

"So, lat's het 'am."

"And," put in Gretchin cheerily, "we can recover the pelts. At least we can do that for the wolves."

Connors looked at her. "The wolves are dead, what defference does et make?" And when there was no reply, "We nade to stake that truck out roight now. The team leader has to decide, but et's what we should do."

As all eyes turned to Martina, Maggie queried, "Dear, what do you think?"

"She's right," was the answer, "and we should start tonight, as soon as we can get out there, really. . . . Gretchin, why don't you and Bradley take a ride out there?"

"Sure. I'll just change. Bradley?"

"Yeah," he replied, "just give me a minute, I'm going to get something else on, too." And wrinkling his nose at Stanley's sandals, he said, "What's the matter, Osipov, the boots too hot? A red cowboy like you shouldn't mind a little Florida heat."

The Russian sighed, wiggling his toes. "Yes, it is a tiny bit too hot for the boots."

"Well, I guess that's understandable, since it's not Vermont or Siberia."

"I will wear them again when summer is over."

With a nod, "Why don't you just take them back to Russia? I won't miss you."

As Bradley pulled up just down the street from the suspected truck Gretchin texted Martina that they were in position. They were facing the semi rig, which had been parked at the curb in the residential area, and could see kids riding bicycles as they played in the street.

Closing the phone, Gretchin said, "You have to run the AC. I'm not rolling my window down out here. Florida mosquitoes are, like, disgusting. They're very powerful."

He smiled to himself. The weakness and extravagance of women always amused him. With a sigh, he switched the engine off, then said, "Don't be a pussy."

"What's that mean?" she returned. "We're going to cook in here, mister, think about it. It's summer, moron." As he made no response, but simply stared through the windshield at the truck, she said fiercely, "I'm hot, turn the goddamn engine on!"

He sighed again, this time heavily. "Yes, ma'am. But you know what gas costs." Then he started the engine and adjusted the vents toward her.

Breathing in the cool air, she said, "Well, I've noticed when we're at home you put premium gas in your precious Corvette."

"Yeah, I wish I had that car now. We'd be nice and cozy together." Then he added, "But maybe not. No, I don't think we would be cozy."

"Look at that," she said, pointing toward the truck. "What is that?"

He opened his phone and activated the quick-dial. "Yeah, Martina? . . . A guy just walked across the street, climbed into the cab, and started the engine. It looks like he's warming it up. . . . I don't know, Martina, it's almost dark. It looks like he's parked directly across the street from the house he came out of."

Gretchin put in, "Tell her I got a pretty good look at him."

"What do you want us to do, Martina? . . . Okay, okay. . . . All right. Bye."

Gretchin waited for him to speak, then said, "Well, smart ass, why not tell me what she said?"

"You want to know what she said? Oh yeah, sure."

"Goddammit, Bradley, don't play with me, tell me what she said."

"Sure. But you don't need to swear at me, I don't appreciate it."

Holding her phone up to him, "See this phone? If you don't tell me right now exactly what Martina said, I'm going to call Connors and tell her what you're doing."

Wearily, "She said they were heading out now and would be here in a few minutes. We're just supposed to follow the truck if it leaves."

Moments later the truck's diesel stacks belched dark exhaust three times and the cab's headlights came on. Then the trailer's orange running lights came on. Following another heavy belch of exhaust, the rig began to move.

"Keep the lights off," she whispered. "Wait till he comes past us."

"I know that, Gretchin, I know what to do."

"We should've parked behind him. Now we have to turn around."

Angrily he snapped, "I *know* that. You saw there wasn't a place, why're you saying that?"

"And," she added nearly frantically, "it's hot as hell, could you turn the air up, stooge?"

Slowly the ominous mass moved toward them. As it crept past he turned his face toward her, as if in conversation. Then quickly he found the back of the rig in his rearview mirror. "All right," he said softly, "now we go."

For five minutes they followed the trailer through the gloom. When the light turned green at the first main intersection the rig crossed the highway and moved into the adjacent residential area. They had not gone far when the truck pulled to the curb.

"Keep back," she warned. Then, "Pull over."

He groaned. "That's about two blocks. Are we gonna walk that? I mean, out in the open?"

"How should I know?"

"You're the one that said to stop."

"I don't know how close we're supposed to get," she returned, "I'm not an expert at this."

"Then why did you say it?"

"To be careful. What, you don't think we should be careful?"

"Within reason, yeah. But I don't just blurt out for someone to pull over."

Her phone vibrated and she opened it. "Yes. . . . Yes, we've stopped. . . . Whittaker, I think. The cross was Whittaker and Terrell. . . . Yeah, it's really kind of the sticks. I mean, it's still residential, but kind of spread-out. There're curbs and sidewalks though. . . . Yeah, I can see the truck. . . . Yeah. . . . Okay. . . . So, just come up the other end of Whittaker. You'll see the truck. . . . Okay, Martina. Good luck."

"So they're close?"

"She said they were really close and just turning onto Whittaker."

"Okay," he said, "yeah, I see their lights now, that must be them. Yeah, they're pulling over. Good grief, they're close. Why so close? I'm moving up, too."

At about a hundred feet from the truck, he pulled to the side, dropped their windows, and shut the engine off.

Then she spoke into the phone, "Yes. . . . Sure."

"What did she say?"

"She said to pull up to about thirty feet behind the truck and leave the engine running but the lights off."

He looked at her. "That's suicide. Osipov's telling her what to say, I know it. She wouldn't have said it like that."

"What's the difference? Just do it. She said *now*."

"Okay." He pulled up closer to the truck and left the engine running. He was sweating and could hear himself breathing. Then on impulse he checked the mirror. "Uh-oh," he whispered, then a little louder, "Uh-oh, somebody's behind us right now. Put the phone down. Just be cool."

Within seconds a man's shadowy face appeared at her window, and she caught her breath. But in response the SUV had pulled up more and now stopped just across from the truck's cab.

"Hey there," the man drawled, "whyn't y'all get outta the car?"

She swallowed. "I was just callin' my mom," she said feebly.

Instantly he put a small revolver to her head and said across to Bradley, "Get out now, boy, or I'll kill 'er."

She watched him straighten up and pull the gun back as they got out. Closing her door, she just caught the wraith-like form of Connors as she opened her door, stepped quickly forward, and laid a rifle along the SUV's hood.

"Whyn't y'all come in the house?" he drawled as Bradley came up beside her. Menacingly he put the gun in her face.

"Sure," she said, unable to breathe. Then, as if in stopped time, she saw the side of his neck blow out, simultaneously heard the shock-blast from Connors' rifle, and watched as he dropped from her vision. When she looked down she could see that his head had been nearly separated from his body and that the gun was still in his hand. "God!" she exclaimed in shock. "God!"

"Get your gun," Bradley ordered, drawing his from under his windbreaker, moving across the yard toward the open door of the garage. Then he heard the SUV roar and watched it speed along the side of the house toward the backyard. Deftly he retrieved an extra magazine and clutched it ready in his free hand.

Martina, Maggie and Connors, guns out, were beside him, and he called back to Gretchin, "Stay with the car. Get inside."

Connors, who had replaced the rifle with a short shotgun, strode quickly out in front as they entered the dark garage. "Give me some loight!" she barked.

Maggie trained her LED on the door to the house. She heard men yelling inside, which made her heart pound, and then was nearly driven backward by two quick blasts from the muzzle of Connors' shotgun as she fired at the latch—*Whop! Whop!*

Connors grabbed the door with her free hand and wrenched it open, and they followed her into the dark house. As they stepped up into the kitchen the lights came on, and a man in Bermuda shorts appeared in the doorway. He yelled for them to get out, and Connors fired into his chest, blowing him backward into a hallway. Stepping over him, as though she had done such a thing many times, she called out, "Packard, get the back, get the back!" Then the popping of at least ten heavy shots came from the back of the house, and she stopped in the dark hallway and ordered, "Give me loight."

But then Packard's voice came rasping through the house, "It's me, Packard, hold up on the lead."

Then Connors stepped forward into the living room, where a wretched chandelier shone down upon a disarray of cardboard boxes, computers, and a desk covered with papers, cups, and food trays.

Entering from the other end of the room, Packard announced, "There's no basement here. Florida's too sandy for basements."

As Packard and Connors searched the rest of the house Bradley left to check on Gretchin. In less than a minute Connors, resting the shotgun upon her shoulder, and Packard, clasping the magnum like a shop tool, returned. To Martina, the dull light from the chandelier gave the two a ghostly appearance. But then, she considered, the whole scene seemed eerie, like perdition might be.

"All roight, team leader," said Connors to Martina, with a grin, "we're done. So, give us some orders or we'll stay the noight."

Bobbie Lee set her pitcher of iced tea upon the patio table. "This place," she said, "is a paradise. The Agency could sure jist leave me here. Hell, I'd retire right now and jist put my feet up."

Bradley, with a grim chuckle, returned, "Well, I'm not sure it would be entirely safe to retire here, not after what we did at that house."

"I don't think anybody's gonna bother y'all here," she returned. "Unless, of course, y'all go out again a-wreakin' more havoc."

Martina lowered her book at this levity. It was now more than a week since Kessler had called to say the clean-up crew had finished at the house and that the project was considered completed. Yet still they were all trying to relax. All, that is, except for Connors and Packard, who were clearly treating the whole gory thing as though it had been just another job.

"Now, Bobbie Lee," replied Maggie, closing her magazine, "why would we be out making enemies?"

"Goodness knows. Hey, people, it's almost five o'clock, and here's my Lasagne bubblin' hot and waitin' for y'all. So, come on and eat, don't insult me."

"You know, Maggie," said Martina, adding sugar to her tea, "I never would have thought five years ago I would be where I am today."

"Oh God, I agree, dear."

After everyone, including Packard, had taken a place at the table, Bobbie Lee cut the Lasagne and placed the portions on the plates as they were passed. "This is real nice," she said, pulling her chair in and reaching for her tea. "We're gittin' to be quite a family here."

"Hey, Packard," said Bradley, "how come you're not sitting by yourself? You're getting to be a regular socialite."

A grim smile. "I have no idea what you're talking about, bub."

"Bradley," said Gretchin, "you talk too much."

Dismissing her with a wave, he turned to the Russian. "Osipov, where do you think they'll send us next, Moscow?"

But Gretchin said, "Would you stop, please, Bradley? You're ruining my dinner, for God's sake."

He pulled his fork from his mouth and chewed happily. Then he swallowed and said to her, as if he had rehearsed it, "I have no concern for what you say. I do not care about you."

Maggie chuckled. "You seemed to care about her the other evening, when she was alone at the car. Why was that?"

"I was concerned about the car, because it's a rental."

Reaching for her tea, "Then why did you say 'I'm going to check on Gretchin'?'"

"Did I say that, Maggie? I don't think I said that."

Then Gretchin said, "I don't think you said it, either, Bradley."

Watching him redden at this and Gretchin give him the finger, Connors said, "Don't yous ever get tired? Why don't yous joost go out in the yard there and fuckin' kell each other? You'd be doin' some of us a favor."

Maggie stared at her. "May I ask you something, Kelly, how old were you when you first learned to swear?"

The white shoulders, one of which was marred by the reddish scar from a bullet hole, rose in a shrug. "Maybe two, I t'ink."

"Two?"

"Aye, 'bout when I learned to talk."

"You didn't talk until you were two?"

"No, I refused to. I told me parents I wasn't gonna talk until I could swear."

"Do all Irish people swear?"

With another shrug, "Et's, loike, en the blood. Et comes from bein' paersecuted, I t'ink."

"Oh."

When Bobbie Lee brought out a hot cherry pie for dessert, she said, "Now, y'all don't have to eat this here pie, but I'm writin' down the name of anybody that doesn't. And if any of y'all breaks a tooth on a cherry pit, I'm not drivin' you to the dentist, so be careful."

CHAPTER 13

The next evening, Kessler sat in the living room. He had come in by commercial air in the afternoon. A hard-looking agent had driven him to the house for dinner and to give the briefing for the team's next project.

"Well," he said jovially, "here we all are." Then he slurped his coffee, looking around at them. When no one responded, he continued, "And that was a great little dinner there, Bobbie."

The hard-looking agent, who had spoken only once during the meal, to ask for some water, did not chime in. He too drank coffee, but unlike Kessler, whose countenance brightened as he ate or drank, he sat expressionless, his face like cold, well-cured concrete.

"Yes, well," said Kessler after waiting in vain for the agent to offer a perfunctory compliment, "here we all are, and I guess we can get started with the briefing. That sounds kind of military, doesn't it—ha."

Martina crossed her legs. "Paul, anything you want to say, please feel free."

"Certainly, Martina, right, I will, thanks. Okay, we should start by acknowledging the good effort of everyone on this last project. You will all be glad, I'm sure, to hear that the Agency is considering the project officially completed. Now we can move on to other projects. Does that make sense?"

Maggie blinked. "Uh, yes, Paul, it does."

He beamed. "Good, well, here we are, and it looks like the team is growing—in numbers, that is. Actually that's something I want to talk about. I know you folks, you guys—they say that now, don't they, *guys*?—uh, I know you guys all would like the team to stay small. And it is still small. But I want to add, officially add, Kelly and Leonard and also now Bobbie. My feeling is that you all work so well together, it's like magic. So, if the magic grows, just let it grow."

"God, that's corny!" blurted Gretchin. "Magic, rreally?"

He stared at her, then reddened. "I could use another term, Gretchin, but you know what I mean. But what does everyone think? Martina, how about you, what do you think?"

"Uh, well," she began, and then, "why are you being cautious about it, may I ask?"

When his response was not forthcoming Connors put in, "Maybe he doesn't want to pess yous off."

He blinked. "Well, thank you, Kelly, I do want to be cautious." Placing his cup and saucer upon the coffee table, he put his hands together.

Martina smiled. "Why don't you just tell us what's on your mind, Paul?"

With his hands still together, "Yes, sure. Okay, Kelly's right, I don't want to upset you guys. Let me lay it on the table. With the success of this project, my theory has been vindicated, if I can use that term. When I first forwarded my plan to put together a team of nonprofessionally trained agents, my ideas fell under the suspicion of CIA experts. Eventually the plan was approved, but only on a trial basis. With the successful completion of this project, involving two segments, you understand, the Agency has become quite positive. They've even moved for more funding. The team can expand, and we can go ahead with more projects. Very frankly, I am elated. I have not exactly received the full paperwork, but that's typical, reports are always slow in coming. But I suspect from the tenor of their language, that they are about to acknowledge in writing that my theory was correct."

"Congratulations," offered Maggie.

He grinned. "Thanks, Maggie, I'm kind of proud of the accomplishment. Another thing, we can even work internationally."

Uncrossing her legs, Martina queried, "With InterPol?"

"No, screw those bastards," he blurted. But then checking himself, he said, "I mean, of course, that we'll be on our own. And the covers are absolutely perfect. No, InterPol won't even know we exist. It's all perfect."

When there was no response from Martina, Maggie asked, "What else is on your mind, Paul?"

"Well, of course," he replied, his fingers gripping his knuckles, "I want to take things in proper order. The first step is to get the approval of everyone on the team. Do you guys want to expand, and do you want to be assigned more projects? It's really as simple as that."

Bradley leaned forward. "Who, may I ask, Paul, will be the team leader?"

"Uh, that will be Martina. I don't want that to change, that's working."

Nodding, Bradley sat back and gave his pants a swipe, as if to brush some lint from them. "And how about Osipov here? His sympathies are still not completely with America, if I can say it. I'm sorry, Stanley, really, but I have to say it. No offense."

The Russian merely smiled.

Kessler, with obvious restraint, replied, "But I knew that. That's actually the way I want it to be. It fits perfectly into the dynamic of the team. Everyone is integral to this dynamic just the way he or she is."

Folding his arms, Bradley gave a nervous shrug. "Okay, fine, that's okay with me."

Gretchin, a contemptuous look on her face, queried, "And you're getting at what, Bradley?"

"What's the difference?" he shot back.

"It was Stanley," she said with a roll of her eyes, "who popped the first bitch. Think about it. Why would he do that? You haven't shot anybody, Bradley, you just sit back and shit-talk people."

His voice rose to a shout. "I do not. And you haven't shot anybody, either, Gretchin."

Cringing visibly, Kessler threw his hands up. "If I may say something, please? Let's calm down. Now, the way I've laid things out is the way I would like them to be. If anyone here doesn't wish to comply with that, now is the time to speak up."

Bradley gave a quick wave. "No, I'm fine, Paul, everything's okay by me. I just thought I'd bring it up. Forget it."

Kessler looked at him for a moment, then said, "Okay. All I need, then, is verbal approval from everyone. One by one, please, you can just say *yes* or *no*. And of course, there'll be no hard feelings if anyone says no. It'll be okay, really, we can work something out. But you have to speak up, because I'm going to take you at your word."

Immediately Bradley sat up straight. "Yes. I'm in. Everything's okay with me."

"Yes, for me," said Gretchin.

Pleasantly Maggie said, "Yes."

With a nod, Martina chimed, "Yes, of course."

Stanley stretched his legs out. "My answer, too, is yes."

Kessler turned to Connors, who apparently saw no need to provide an answer. "Kelly?"

She gave a simple nod.

He hesitated. "Can I hear it, please?"

"Sher, why the fuck not?"

He closed his eyes for a moment, but then turned to Packard. "Leonard?"

Wearily the other grunted, "Yeah."

Kessler looked at him. "You got enough space to breathe, Leonard?" When there was no reply, he said, "Like the rest of us, Mr. Packard here values his privacy. ... And now that leaves you, Ms. Henry. Want to join the team officially?"

"Sure. Everyone seems to like my pie."

Following a general chitter of laughter, he said, raising his cup to look for a last bit of coffee, "Don't let her fool you, my friends. She was very tough in Memphis, I understand. She grabbed a motorcycle, chased three carjackers, and at eighty miles an hour shot and killed the driver. And when the car stopped rolling, she killed the second one and then with her pistol beat the last one to death. ... We're fortunate to have her with us."

"Well," she drawled, "I did break my hand on the guy. I was out of ammo."

Everyone looked at the figure of Bobbie Lee Henry as she stood slouched against the door-frame, a dishtowel stuffed into her waistband. The plain, honest expression on her face seemed particularly disarming. And although they were used to seeing her in the skimpy T-shirt and shorts, none except Connors had until then taken full notice of her rippling, rocky muscles.

Suddenly Kessler looked at his watch, then got up. "Well, I've got to get going here, back to the airport. I'll see everyone in Philadelphia." He watched impatiently while the agent slowly rose to his feet. "Everybody might as well pack up here. Give it a couple more days and then come on home. I'll see you all when you get back. Glad nobody got hurt."

"But, Paul," said Martina, "wasn't this to be a briefing?"

"Oh yes. But I'm out of time, sorry. We'll talk about the new project when you're all home."

CHAPTER 14

Philadelphia, September

Gretchin twisted the top to the India ink, put the bottle into her pen-and-ink box, and looked at the wet drawings. Already their edges had begun to curl. After drying they could be pressed with weights to flatten them, but for now they must be left to ripple from uneven surface tension produced by paper, ink, and water.

These particular abstracted cityscapes had left her with an upset stomach. But she did not care, for it was so very good to be back in her studio. Perhaps Florida, with its flowering life, had been more beautiful than Philadelphia for her artistic mind, but once inside her studio, her own special place in the universe, neither the flowers nor the sunshine mattered. All that mattered to her psyche was the dream world she moved into through her art.

True, she had come to want something more in life than art. Life seemed cold and sterile, regardless of how many pictures she produced. A painting might suck the emotional life out of her, but it could never take her milk and love her back. But why was she thinking like this at fifty-four?

When her phone chimed she looked at its screen, then opened it. "What? ... Sure. ... Twenty minutes, I guess. I have to wash my hands and change. ... No, it can't be sooner, I also have to pee. Twenty minutes. ... Don't do that, just text me, only pricks honk. ... Okay."

Martina turned the faucet handle until the pressure was gone from the hose, then hung the hose over the elbow Stanley had made for it beside the garage door. It would not be necessary to water the tiny backyard for very much longer, for it was already mid-September.

After locking the back door she made her way past the exercise equipment and climbed the stairs to the kitchen. He was there, eating the potato soup she had made for him.

"This is very good soup," he said.

Washing her hands at the sink, she looked at him. "Does it taste Russian?"

"I think it does, yes."

"It's supposedly from a Russian recipe." She shook the water from her hands, then pulled off a paper towel. "But what do you think, does it remind you of Moscow or the peasants or something else Russian?"

He wrinkled his nose. "I cannot tell."

"The potatoes are from the Russian market you took me to."

"But I am sure they are not really from Russia."

Giving his shoulder a pat, "Well, just use your imagination, then. I have to take a shower. They'll be here in less than an hour."

"Can I imagine you in the shower?"

With another pat, "If you like."

"Another meeting," Kessler said as he took a seat on the couch. "So, this is the notorious couch where Richard sat?"

Maggie held a plate of cookies before him. "Yes, it is. And that is the door by which he left and never came back."

"Doors are like that," he said.

"Yes," she replied, and when he had chosen a cookie, "they are like the choices we make."

He took a bite, then smiled. "I think I chose the right cookie."

"So, Paul," Martina said at length, "do you want to tell us about the next project?"

"I do, yes," he replied. "And I think everyone will be pleased. How would you all like to go to Texas?"

When no one responded, Gretchin queried, "You're making it sound like a vacation."

"Not quite," he chuckled as he opened the case and retrieved two eight-by-ten color prints. "Just pass these around. These two guys, based in Waco, Texas, are in the business of smuggling drugs to China, no less. Now, the Agency isn't concerned about the drugs, but we are concerned about the commercial atmosphere between the U.S. and China. Here's what we think is happening. Political entities in Mexico are attempting to divert U.S. business from China to Mexico. That whole world of commerce between countries is pretty complex, and the Agency doesn't want to get into the mix to any significant depth. The drugs are being sent from Mexico to a U.S.-based entity that then smuggles them in huge quantities into China, especially to cities and even to specific areas where U.S. businesses operate. The Mexicans believe that the negative effect, however slow, will certainly turn U.S. businesses toward Mexico."

Martina crossed her legs. "Let me guess," she said, "the whole thing is getting muddied with blood, which could bring the U.S. into a lose-lose situation."

"Correct. The U.S. smugglers, paid by the Mexicans, have hit it somewhat big time and have turned violent and become extremely dangerous. Numerous murders have occurred. So, now it's not just the Mexicans screwing with U.S. relations with China, it's the smugglers screwing with U.S. relations with both countries. The Agency now considers the situation to be toxic. Enough said."

The Russian queried, "Is it just these two guys, and do you have more pictures?"

"No other photos, sorry, and it's just these two guys, we think. But even as we speak they could be bringing other people in. A key element for us is time. Texas is the largest exporting state, which means the authorities are looking for stuff like this all the time. If we don't get these guys now, Texas authorities might actually incarcerate them for something, which would be very bad, considering the malignant contacts they could make in prison. They were both in prison before getting into the smuggling. If they get in again, with what and who they know on the outside and with the connections they can make in prison, when they come out they'll start a veritable mafia. And then it'll take more than a team to stop them, it'll take the Marines. Let's not let it get there."

"Well," quipped Bobbie Lee, flexing her muscles, "I've seen it before, myself, that sometimes puttin' people in prison can be harder on society than jist leavin' them out."

Kessler nodded appreciatively. "But with these guys neither option is on the table."

Martina cleared her throat. "So, when do we start, Paul?"

Puffing his cheeks, he thought for a moment. "Actually, tomorrow would be optimal, but it's going to take the Agency about a week to put it together. It wouldn't be a problem to get one person or even two down there by tomorrow, but working out the logistics for a team like this can be quite complex. But we'll work out the basic transportation and housing, the entrance and exit strategies, and moving the considerable firepower you'll need. Most likely the team will leave in five or six days. But anything can happen, and I would say you should all be ready to go within two days and upon a two-hour notice."

Connors grinned. "Don't forgat there moight be more'n two people we have to deal weth."

"Exactly. Which means they might come after you. We'll remember to factor that in, of course, Kelly. We should all exercise caution."

"Oh, I'm always cautious," she returned, "cautious to kell ever' fuckin' one of 'am so's there's nobody to come after me."

He swallowed hard. "I understand your, uh, perspective, your approach, Kelly, but I meant caution in relation to the safety of the team. We don't want to lose any of you."

"I'm touched."

As if perplexed, he simply stared at her.

"T'at's et, isn't et?" she continued. "You know, don't ever touch a gun. We don't touch guns, do we? And ef you see a gun, tell a policeman. And the adults who must carry the derty t'ings always have their fengers outsoide the tregger guard. We must be safe, musn't we?"

"What are you getting at, Kelly? We *do* want to be safe, don't we?"

"Oh, sher," she replied, "so's we don't shoot each other." She gave him a moment to chuckle, for she knew he would. When he did she gave him a serious look, which sobered him. Then she said, "I'm not sayin' I want to be shot. Et hurts to be shot. I've been shot so many fuckin' toimes I, loike, can't count. I'm startin' to walk funny joost from all the muscle destruction. But en this work, too much safety can gat you kelled. A lot of the people we're dealin' weth are experts weth weapons, and et's better to joost gat en there and put tham down queck at any cost. And ef you're worryin' about your own safety, they'll gat you while you're worryin'. You can't be t'inkin' of safety, you have to be t'inkin' of kellin'."

He blinked, as if to consider this. Then he said, "Yes, I understand, but I would suggest that maybe Maggie or Martina or Gretchin, who are not as experienced and, um, how should I say it, as aggressive as you are, would be better off being a little more safety conscious."

"I'm sayin' et would be better for tham joost to wise up queck. Be aggrassive, put the fenger en the tregger guard, on the tregger, and keep et there, and shoot to fuckin' kell every fuckin' toime."

"I am thinking," said the Russian, as if to everyone, "that I am in agreement with her."

Gretchin, recalling that she would have been dead if Connors' had hesitated placing that shot in the Florida raid, said, "Actually, Kelly, I think I sympathize with your viewpoint. The wising up and aggression, well, I'm going to have to work at, but I'll try."

"Kelly's right," growled Packard, sending a grimace in Kessler's direction, "you can have your safety, teach it to your kids and, I guess, to your professionals."

Kessler gave a grim chuckle. "You're not a professional, Leonard?"

Packard gave him a hard look this time. "You didn't hire me to be an agent, and you know it. If I wanted to be in the Agency like that, I'd go to school, I'd learn a couple new languages, I'd think about making a difference and all that horseshit, instead of just making a hole in somebody's head. I'd be a professional agent, I'd be cautious and think safety, and I'd cry in my soup every time I had to kill somebody. But you didn't hire me to cry in my soup. I'm crotchety, I carry two goddamn canons, and I don't want anybody telling me to be safe."

Bobbie Lee, forefinger out and thumb up to form a gun, chirruped, "Absolutely, I totally agree."

Giving his chin a scratch, Kessler at length replied, "Well, what can I say to that? Except, I suppose, I wish you all good hunting."

Martina cleared her throat, then said, "So, Paul, to recap, we should be ready within two days, but expect to go within a week."

"Right," he replied, glad to be done with the safety discussion, "that's the time frame, I think. I'll be doing most of the organizing, and I'll push, but yeah, you'll probably go in a week. And you shouldn't have to be down there more than a week or two. We know exactly who they are, at least who these two are. But I'll work it all up. . . . I did have something else to discuss though. The new funding from the Agency is sufficient to secure a major relocation for the team. Kelly, Bobbie, you've been staying in Leonard's apartment. How is that working out? Or maybe I should be asking Leonard that."

"I think we're all good, for now," said Bobbie Lee. "We stay out of each other's way."

Kessler gave a nod. "Here's my proposal, then. The Agency will purchase a single facility for the team. That part will be simple and quickly expedited. What will not be simple is finding a facility that accommodates the social dynamic of your group."

"Are you saying, Paul," Martina returned, "that we don't get along very well?"

Smiling, he brought his hands together. "The important thing is that the Agency believes in you.

Of course, *I* believed in you because of my theory, but now they believe in you, too. But of course, the team was *my* idea. Anyway, well, you've performed wonderfully, and they want you to continue. So, they're willing to fund, within reason, whatever works for the team. Here's what I've been thinking. If we buy the farm in Vermont from your sister, Martina, you could all set up there. How does that sound?" When she only looked at him thoughtfully, he added, "I know you like the city, but we've got to get you into a rural situation. If you like, we could acquire a property here in Pennsylvania or even relocate you to the facility in Idaho. But Vermont would work best, I think. There is even a small independent airport not far from the property."

"I'd have to sell everything here," said Bradley. "I couldn't keep up with the stuff, the house, the car, if I wasn't here."

Gretchin said wryly, "Oh, not your Corvette, Bradley."

He looked at her, then turned to Kessler, "All right, I'll do it, I will."

"Stanley and I are positive," was Martina's answer. "Maggie, what about you? As you know, it's cold up there."

A smile. "It's okay with me."

"Fine," said Kessler. "I see a nod from everyone, so I'll put it in motion. Look to relocate as soon as the Texas project is completed. Done. That wasn't so bad." Then he exhaled wearily. "Is there any more coffee? I think I could use another cup."

CHAPTER 15

Waco, Texas

Texas dust blew across the runway as the Twin Otter touched down at the tiny rural airport near Waco. The plane had flown throughout the night, making only two refueling stops. After taxiing around a loop, it came to a halt in front of two black SUVs and a gray sedan.

Three men in windbreakers and ball caps stood waiting. Martina, groggy from the grueling flight, wondered why the uniformity of it all needed to be so obvious. But then, regimentation was like that, she considered, rubbing her weary eyes, it had its place, one often vital, for it produced a certain kind of result that creativity could not. The men looked so robotic, she thought, as they stood there waiting by the SUVs, which practically sang a duet that they were CIA vehicles. All of it displayed the very mechanistic uniformity that the team was not supposed to have. But she was glad to see evidence that the mechanism would be in place for the team's exit when all of this was over and it was time to walk off the stage, because as every intelligent actor knew, a botched exit could ruin the play. She watched as the agents now made their way toward the airplane.

"My goodness, I am tired," Maggie exclaimed softly.

Martina looked at her friend. Her face, which she had always seen as enduringly young, now seemed haggard. "I'm sorry, Maggie. Yes, you do look tired."

Indeed, everyone was tired to the point of fatigue, for no one had slept well. The two one-hour stops to refuel the plane and allow the pilot and passengers to use the restroom and get a bite to eat had refreshed no one, but only made them feel more jerked around. They had been jerked around not only by the air but by the Agency. Although they had spent the allotted week preparing for a variety of possible entrances for the project, which meant leaving Philadelphia by car, bus, and air, their efforts had been wasted. At the last possible minute the plural entrance plan had been scrapped by Kessler in favor of a singular one, so that all commercial reservations had to be cancelled. The Otter had been dispatched to a northeast Philadelphia airport to get the entire team and transport them to Texas.

"God!" exclaimed Gretchin, reaching for the edge of the door to steady herself. "Is this for real? I feel like I've been dragged rather than flown."

Maggie held her stomach as Stanley grabbed her suitcase and set it down on the tarmac. Watching his movements seemed to make her feel worse.

She was still holding her stomach when she climbed into the SUV, put her head back, and closed her eyes. Pulling her purse closer, she realized that it would always now be heavier because of the revolver and speed loaders. She could hear voices as the others unloaded the aircraft. The rear gate was popped open and equipment was loaded into the back. She kept her eyes closed as Connors got in beside her, then Stanley and Martina into the front.

Stanley signaled the three men and then followed their sedan to the highway. He waved as they turned left and drove away. He checked his mirror for Bradley's SUV, then turned right onto the highway and accelerated.

"There is so much ammunition in this car," he said, "anyone would think the Russians were coming."

Martina laughed. "Oh, that is very good, sir. That's right, we first met in a movie store, didn't we?"

"Yes, two spies."

"I was not a spy," she retorted playfully. She loved it when he started a joke. "I was an Advisor, sir."

"Spy."

"No."

"You were the spy, admit it. But I was not spy, I was infiltrator."

"Spy," she returned. "Admit it yourself."

He shrugged. "Okay, we were two spies. Good. This is a heavy car, but still I am feeling the weight in the steering."

"Because of the ammunition?"

"Yes. It was all there when I opened up the back."

"Why did Paul switch on the entrance strategies, do you think? Safety?"

"It was probably for security, like switching credit cards just before paying at store. But this is good, I am thinking. No house, just two hotel rooms, get the work done, and fly out. Very clean. So, I am agreeing with him."

"I think they call them motels down here."

"Yes," he chuckled, "I have heard this. Motels are usually only used for three illicit things—cheap sex, cheap sleep, and cheap criminal activity."

"Which do you think we're going to do?"

He grinned. "Maybe all three."

"Is Bradley still behind us?"

"Yes. I see him. He is staying close. Just make sure I do not make a wrong turning."

"*A wrong turn*," she corrected, looking down at the hand-written directions. "You're fine. Just stay on this highway for about two more miles."

When they pulled into the Cactus Motor Inn they parked at numbers six and seven, according to Kessler's instructions. The gleaming black finish of the SUVs contrasted sharply with the moribund paint of the motel. The old buildings, like painted cardboard boxes, seemed dried and withered from the Texas sun.

"Good Lord," said Gretchen as she got out of Bradley's SUV, "this place looks more like Mexico, where's my sombrero? And I suppose there will be flies and snakes."

"Don't be negative," he returned, pulling the car's rear gate open.

"What time is it? Did it change?"

"It did."

"God, what a drab place."

"Just go in, I'll get the suitcases. Martina said they have a little Mexican restaurant."

"Ah, cuisine."

"By the way," she said without looking at him, "do I sleep with Bobbie Lee or Packard?"

"You don't want to sleep with me?" And after her look of disgust, "I'm shocked."

"Don't be. God, this place is plain." And in singsong, "Somebody needed an artist."

Bobbie Lee grabbed a suitcase. "Hey, come on, this place is exotic. Hope they have chili and beer."

From the office a tall, skinny man emerged, pulled on a wide-brimmed hat, and strode toward them. The heels of his lizard boots scuffed as he walked, and he sported a Colt in a crossdraw holster.

"Hey there," he said, "I'm Ted. You folks're all registered, and I brought your keys. They's plenty a room in there. These bungalows look small, but they's double apartments in each one, that's four apartments, and each double apartment has a kitchen. You can really spread out. I've had you folks in before, so I know what your gonna ask, and no, you cain't see your cars from the road. This ain't no Mickey Mouse place. I'm kinda proud of it. They's cable and we used to have a swimmin' pool. Now we've got a Mexican restaurant. Here's your keys. You can come and go as you want, any hour. I spoke to Mr. Kessler, who made all the arrangements. Everything's paid for, so don't pay me when you leave. Just leave the keys in the rooms and go. And now I'll stop talkin', and that ain't easy for me to do. And one more thing, I know you change your own linens and you don't wanna be disturbed. Gotcha."

Martina responded meekly, "We appreciate that. And thank you for welcoming us to Texas."

He took his hat off, and making no attempt to disguise the glimmer in his eyes as he looked at her hair, he said, "Well, it's pretty here. You've come at a good time. The beginnin' of a Texas fall is a little like the beginnin' of a Texas spring, real beautiful, like your hair, lady."

Then he pulled the hat on, tugged once at the brim, and with a smile and a nod, turned and walked back to the office.

Toward evening, after everyone had tried to sleep, they walked over to the restaurant. They waited while four tables were placed together to form a square and then covered with a checkered tablecloth. As they pulled their chairs up the waiter handed out menus and assured them that everything on the list was *genuine Mexico y no loco.*

"Did you see those boots?" Maggie queried Stanley. "They're even fancier than yours."

"I was looking at them. I was going to offer the trade of mine for his, but I did not want to be rejected."

Martina looked across at them. She liked it when they joked. She wondered at the beneficence of nature, how it had given this woman to be her dearest friend and this man to be her husband. And more, life had given her all these people, not merely as colleagues and comrades, but as brothers and sisters. Around these tables pushed together to form one table and covered with one cloth were gathered her brothers and sisters in arms, her family. And the candle burning in its little glass jar at the center of the table, what was that but a symbol of their heart, their intellect, their determining will?

"What shall we talk about tonight?" she asked aloud.

"Well," offered Bradley, "we could talk about Corvettes."

Gretchin lowered her menu. "Thank you for that, Lancelot."

"You know," he returned, "the name *Gretchin* sounds a little like *Guinevere*, don't you think?"

"Maybe a little," said Stanley.

"So, what gallant act would Guinevere suggest I perform?"

Without looking up from the menu, "I'd like to see you throw yourself on your sword, but then who would drive the fucking car?"

"Cute," he said, giving the table a slap, "you've got to be nasty, don't you? I ask you to name something gallant, and you suggest suicide. How stupid is that? All right, you're a lousy Guinevere—it's back to Gretchin for you."

Martina sighed heavily. "Could we talk about something else?"

CHAPTER 16

Toothbrush in hand, Bobbie Lee switched off the bathroom light, then popped it back on when she saw Packard in the hallway.

"Thanks much," he rasped. Then he queried, "Why do you like the 19?"

"I d'know, jis' used to it, 'guess, and I don't mind six shots. I kinda like the balance, it feels real good in my hand."

"Good answer. Go with the ergonomics, you gotta feel comfortable with the iron."

She looked at the plain shirt, the holster straps exaggerating the bend of the shoulders, the gun butts. She wondered if he sometimes slept in the rig. He reminded her so much of Dad, who seemed always to have the rifle in his hand at home. Dad made her feel secure, for she had seen him shoot, but Mama made fun of him, calling him a gangster and swearing to everyone that he was paranoid.

"But I like .357," she said. "I can't git away from it as the final word in all-around ballistics."

"No argument there. Thirty-eight's a smidgen light when you need a punch. Forty-one mag ammo costs so much to shoot that you can't even practice with the stuff. And .44 mag? I don't know, the flinch factor throws me off every time. Not worth it. But .357—perfect, absolutely perfect."

"I tried seven-shot wheels, but didn't like 'em, cylinder turn seemed a little slow and labored. But that was with smaller frames. The 686 I tried, like yours, seemed about right."

"Well, a seven wheel is slower than a six, but I'll take the extra shot."

She raised a forefinger. "Fourteen."

With a grin, "That's right, I've got two. God, they're heavy by the end of the day."

"What do you do 'bout the ammo?"

He took his eyes from her robe. "Speed loaders in a suit pocket usually. I used to carry it loose, clicking around in my pocket. I'd tell the kids I had a pocketful of jellybeans. One kid reached in, grabbed a few bullets, and I had to yell at him to give me back my jellybeans. But yeah, speed loaders kind of rescued me from all that, and they're a lot faster."

"You've got a great rig there. D'you ever take it off?"

A chuckle. "I do wash, if that's what you mean. The truth is, yeah, sometimes I sleep with it." His eyes went to her robe again. She seemed so plainly pretty, so honest, standing there with her hands shoved deep into the cushy pockets. "I'll bet you've got your hand on your P-64 right now," he said.

"I'm not bettin." And she pulled out the gun, her finger on the trigger.

He nodded, scratching his ear. "Surplus, right?"

"Yep. I don't know why I carry it, there are a lot better guns out there now. Dad used to take me to the shows, and the only thing I had money for as a kid was the surplus stuff. Even now cold war guns fry my circuits. I actually got this when I was a kid and jist got used to it. It's skinny and kicks like hell, but it's got a great trigger. The 9x18's not a big boy, but I feel comfortable with it as a backup."

He listened until he became aware that he was staring. Then he cleared his throat and said that he'd better get going. When she said good night and shuffled away in her slippers, he let his eyes follow her.

Martina watched his hands as he checked the half-cock on the Tokarev and then grabbed the Makarov to bring it to bed. She considered this Stanley Osipov to be a beautiful man with graceful movements. She pictured him firing the pistol. But then she felt a pang, for in many ways she had caused him to exchange his camera for a gun.

"What is Connors shouting about?" he asked, lifting the covers to get into bed.

"I have no idea, I haven't been able to follow the conversation."

"It is because the wall is plaster."

"She's been ranting about something for probably ten minutes. Poor Maggie. But they like each other, so I'm sure it's okay. Come here, give me a hug. I think I need my back rubbed by those Russian hands."

"For when do I set the alarm?"

"Oh, make it eight. We're all still pretty tired from the flight, and Paul said to rest a couple of days anyway. Tomorrow we'll sort the ammunition, check the equipment, stuff like that. Everybody needs the rest. Is your phone set to text the pilot if mine fails?"

"Yes, my dear leader lady, it is."

"Good. Now please kiss me." And after he did, she said dreamily, "The tacos were so good tonight, weren't they?"

"Yes, but the spices might not let you sleep."

"Then I'll be awake and will need someone to hold my hand."

"I will be here."

"Boy, you two sure fight a lot," said Bobbie Lee, passing a black-with-sugar to Bradley and a cream-with-sugar to Gretchin. "Git your stuff, ever'body. I think it's all here."

Earlier, before anyone was up, she had gone out for groceries and produce, as she intended to put a salad together. Fortunately the menu of the Mexican restaurant was fairly extensive, making only minor provisions necessary. She had taken a list for snack requests, and had picked up coffee and doughnuts on her return trip.

Nearly everyone was awake when she brought the groceries in. Only Martina and Stanley were still asleep. Maggie and Connors had gone out for a walk, Packard had found a sports channel on the TV, and Gretchin and Bradley were disputing the possession of a TV programming guide.

She put the things away and began to wash the lettuce. She liked these people, with their chatter and their idiosyncrasies. If she had a social talent at all, it was reading people. She could not read minds the way a psychologist could, but she could read people. And these people, despite their quirks, she had found generally to be straight shooters.

She had learned from her parents that there was nothing so important to be found in the human makeup as truth. Truth could take many forms, but always it was recognizable. It might take the form of faithfulness or candor or bitter outrage, but never did it take the form of a lie. She had been raised to despise, even to hate, if necessary, those who lied. Personal integrity was everything. You could be wrong, but you couldn't lie. Your speech could be foul, but it couldn't be false. And if all humanity lived behind a mask, none of humanity, not one single person, no matter how clever, could work evil behind that mask for very long before being discovered. Like truth, a lie could take many forms, but ultimately it would always be recognizable.

During the afternoon she helped Stanley break out the ammunition. For herself, she took a box of Makarov ball and two boxes of .357 magnum. The bulk of the supply was for those who would be the first to go in. But her extensive knowledge of weapons and her work for the Memphis police had earned her the respect of everyone on the team, and all wished her in the fray.

When everyone walked to the restaurant for dinner, Connors queried her privately, "What do you t'ink of this group?"

"It's a great group," she replied. "Could've used 'em in Mimphis." But giving her nose a scratch,

"I'm guessin', if there's a weakness in the team it's Bradley."

"Not the Russian?"

"Oh, no, not him. Pure as shit. That guy's a rebel, if I ever saw one."

A nod. "I t'ink you're roight. Joost wanted to gat your opinion."

"But I'm guessin', Killy," she added, watching as the others disappeared into the restaurant, "that even Bradley wouldn't sell out in a pinch. He might in the small things and maybe in some of the big things, but in a fight I think he'd stay the course. He can aggravate you, 'cause he's like a kid can be sometimes. And he's kind of a fool most of the time. But in my judgment, he'd take a bullet for anybody on the team, includin' Gritchin, in a little bitty heartbeat. I think he likes her anyway, but don't quote me on that."

Connors nodded again. "Aye, chemistry's a weird t'ing."

"It is, to be sure, and that's a fact."

"He's set his eyes on me, loike, a couple of toimes."

"Well, I assume he's got a dick, and if he's got one it's gonna give 'im trouble. Men are like that, they git aggrissive."

"He's got one all roight, I saw et when I was walkin' by his room."

"There'ya go, then. It's gonna give 'im trouble."

"I'm not worried 'bout hem, I'm worried 'bout me. He's put his eyes on me, but ef he gats his deck out around me, I'll prob'ly, loike, joost fuckin' shoot hem."

Two days later, Stanley and Bradley serviced the SUVs and then, with Bobbie Lee's help, loaded them.

"She is strong," said Stanley.

"Yeah," returned Bradley, "look at those muscles. She sure doesn't wear perfume though, does she?"

The Russian looked at him. "She does not smell bad, she smells like woman."

"Speak for yourself. I think a little perfume would help. But looking at those muscles tells me I should start lifting weights again."

"I admire her."

"Why?"

With a shrug, "I have always admired strong women."

"Good for you, pal. I guess I don't share your sentiments. But I can sure see her beating a man to death with those hands. Don't cross her, right?"

Surveillance on the previous day had confirmed the Agency's intel describing a small warehouse along the main highway leading to the city. Numerous cars, two box trucks, and a motorcycle had been noted. According to the latest information from Kessler, two new hires, a man and a woman, both probably Mexican, had taken place. They were not to be considered as targets. Since the cover business saw limited but somewhat steady customer traffic, caution was to be exercised not to involve the public.

When the vehicles had been readied, Bobbie Lee prepared a quick lunch, and the team sat down to discuss the final plan. Stanley's SUV, with Martina as navigator and Connors and Bobbie Lee, would approach first. Bradley's, with Gretchin as navigator and Packard and Maggie, would hang back at the shoulder of the highway. Initially Connors was to go to the office with a phony highway survey concerning sidewalks. But as her accent was so heavy, it was decided that Bobbie Lee should accompany her and do the talking. Once inside, Connors would decide when to move. Upon their entrance, Bradley's SUV would roll past the first and drive to the loading dock at the back.

At the first sound of shots, of course, they were all to go into action to destroy the targets. No one else was to be considered a target, except upon threat. Stanley, leaving Martina to drive in an emergency, would go in to back up Connors and Bobbie Lee. Packard and Bradley would enter through the rear, leaving Gretchin in the SUV to drive, if necessary, and Maggie to handle emergency phone communications.

Toward the middle of the afternoon, with a Texas sun bathing everything in yellow, Stanley turned into the driveway leading to the warehouse. Unconsciously he thumbed the Makarov's safety to make sure it was off, then leaned forward to make sure the Tokarev was on half-cock at the small of his back. Just in front of the warehouse office, still quite visible from the highway less than two hundred feet away, he pulled to a stop and let the engine idle.

"Tell her that we are going to go in now," he said, his eyes on the office door.

Softly she spoke, "They're going in, Gretchin. Stay with me on the phone. . . . Sure. Okay, here we go."

Connors and Bobbie Lee opened their doors, got out, and began walking toward the door. The latter clasped a clipboard. Before taking the step to the porch they stopped, and Bobbie Lee walked a few feet away to get a better view of the motorcycle parked at the side of the building.

"What is she doing?" Stanley whispered.

Martina blinked. "She's looking at the motorcycle. She's pointing and saying something about it to Connors."

"No," he muttered in unbelief, "she should just go to the door."

Then the two women stepped gingerly onto the porch and approached the door. Connors pressed the buzzer. Momentarily a man's face appeared in the upper portion of the storm door, then the door was pushed open. Stanley, his window down, could now hear what he was saying. He could also hear the cars running along the highway.

"Yes, can I help you?" the man asked.

Bobbie Lee cleared her throat. "Yessir," she drawled. "We're from the Department of Highways, and we're gonna start assayin' the area to put in sidewalks along the highways, in front of all the businesses in this area."

"Yes?"

"Well, sir, we have a survey we need to show you and all the businesses in the area, that you need to look at and fill out. It's very short. Can we come in an' show it to you? It'll just take a second, then we can jist leave it and pick it up tomorrow."

"You can just leave it with me," he said.

"Well, sir, we'd like to explain it, we're supposed to explain it. It'll jist take a second. Say, is that your Bonneville out there? I love motorcycles."

He grinned and pushed the door wider. They could all clearly now identify him as one of the targets.

"Yeah, that's mine," he said.

Waving the clipboard flamboyantly, she burst out, "God, that is a beautiful bike. You're a lucky man. That's a 750, right? Still with carburetion, and you've got a kick on it. Damn."

"That's right," he chuckled. "I'm kind of a manual guy, I don't like electrics." And giving his head a shake, he pronounced, "That's a bike, ladies, that's a bike."

"Well, hell, step on out here and show it to me, wouldya? You're a dude to have a motorcycle like that. They're hot in Florida, boy, I seen 'em down there. I love Triumphs. Used to have a 650, myself."

As he followed them from the porch he began to laugh, popping his hands together. "It'll go a hundred. Even more. One time, I hit a rock in the road, just a rock, not too big, I guess. Took flight, sailed about fifty feet, came down smooth as shit. The thing's like an airplane. Yep, it's jus' me and the bike, out there." He held up a forefinger. "That's one helluva bike."

She grinned. "I believe it, sir."

"This thing hauls ass, lemme tellya. You're lookin' at the real deal, right there."

"I believe it, sir, I do," she said. "I see you even keep your key in the ignition."

"Hey, faster getaways. Rock and roll." Then he queried Connors, "How 'bout you? You like bikes, too?"

Connors merely nodded.

Instantly Bobbie Lee raised the clipboard. "Well, sir, lemme jist come inside here and explain what you need to fill out. Come on."

She stepped onto the porch and pulled the door open. He followed, and as he stepped through the doorway, she queried, "You got any business partners around? They'll need to listen up, too."

"Yeah. Yeah, come on in," he said.

When Connors had followed them inside and closed the door Martina said into the phone, "They're in."

Moments later, Bradley's SUV moved around them and rolled along beside the building toward the back.

"I am holding my breath," whispered Stanley.

"I know."

"Do you see them?"

"I can't see anything, Stanley. That window's pretty big, so they must have gone into another room, I think." Then she said, "What's that?"

A car coming from the highway moved around them and came to a stop in one of the customer parking spaces. Rolling down her window, the driver lit a cigarette and exhaled smoke to the outside. Beside her a little girl rolled her window down, too. Then the woman got out, the cigarette dangling from her lips.

"I'm gonna ask 'em if we can use the bathroom here," she drawled, slinging her purse over a shoulder. "You two stay in the car."

The back of a boy's head then appeared in the rear window. As the woman, evidently their mother, took another drag at the cigarette multiple shots rang out from inside the building and a hole was blasted out of the window.

"Oh no," breathed Martina.

"Take the steering wheel," Stanley said, getting out.

Quickly she slid behind the wheel, then spoke into the phone, "We've got a problem, the public's here, be careful. They're firing inside. Stanley's going in, . . . he's reaching for the Tokarev."

Stepping to the porch, the Russian barked to the woman, "Get back into car!" But she only looked at him, as if in disbelief, her eyes wide, the cigarette still in her lips. Now the Tokarev was out, and he pulled the door open and entered.

The room was empty, so he moved toward an open door, the gun aloft. He heard Connors shouting and then shots erupted from the next room, many shots. Crouching, he entered the room and instantly guns were fired all around him. *Whop! Whop! Whop! Whop! . . . Pop! Pop! Pop!* Then he saw that someone was firing down the stairway from the second floor. Connors, pushing a desk aside, stood up, gun in hand, and resolutely began climbing the stairs, into the firing.

Then she fired, again and again and again as shots were fired at her down the stairway. Again she fired. *Bam! Bam! Bam! Bam! Bam!*

Instantly Stanley moved up behind her. "I am behind you, Connors," he said clearly.

She did not turn, but continued firing. As she crouched to pop out a mag and snap in another he fired up the stairway.

"What the fuck!" she exclaimed at the Tokarev's huge blast. "Fuckin' cannon!"

As they neared the landing the firing down the stairway halted, and they could hear Bobbie Lee, who had gone in pursuit into another room on the first floor, yelling ferociously, "Bastard! Bastard!" Stepping onto the landing, they heard more shots behind them from Bobbie Lee's direction. Then they heard her voice as she came up behind Stanley, "What a bastard, tried to trick me. I shot 'im in the goddamn head, the bastard, the fucking bastard."

Connors then, her gun straight out, stepped into the room from which the man had been firing. But the room was empty. Then multiple shots erupted outside, and there was yelling and then automatic fire.

"Shet," she uttered, "they're usin' real stuff out there." Then she stepped to an open window and looked down. "He's joomped," she muttered.

Martina, who had seen the man jump, was now out of the SUV. Oddly, the mother backed away from her and just stood there smoking, her eyes still wide. As the man ran toward the woman Martina leveled the .38, closed an eye, and threw two shots at him—*Blop! Blop!* But the shots went wide, and the man, ignoring Martina, slapped the woman to the ground and clambered into her car.

"Get out, bitch!" he croaked at the little girl, putting his gun to her head. Instantly she pulled the latch, got out, faced him, then began to back away, staring at him. He turned the key, pulled the shift, backed the car with a screech, then put the accelerator down and roared past the SUV and drove out onto the highway. He had not seen the little boy in the back seat.

Packard and Bradley, attempting to enter the building through a back door, had pulled an outer door open and were inside an alcove when a man with an autopistol and a woman with a revolver attacked Maggie and Gretchin seated in the SUV, blowing their windows in but missing both women. Instantly and virtually simultaneously Packard and Bradley whirled and fired from the alcove, and Maggie and Gretchin fired from the windowless SUV, all throwing multiple shots at the attackers. The four continued firing even as both attackers dropped. Then Packard reached for a speedloader and walked over to the bodies. Twisting the bullets home, he looked down at the man. Kicking the autopistol away, he cocked the magnum, put it to the man's head, and fired— *Shlam!*—blowing a corner of the forehead from the skull. With a grunt of satisfaction, he turned to the woman, whose hand still clasped the revolver.

"Let me do it," said Bradley, leveling the .45 from ten feet away. As the other backed up, Bradley fired twice.

Neither Maggie nor Gretchin had been seriously hurt, but both blotted blood from cuts to neck and face caused by flying glass. Then Maggie's phone vibrated, and she read aloud Martina's text to come around to the front of the building.

When Packard and Bradley immediately began to walk Gretchin dropped the bloody tissue, pulled the shift down, and brought the SUV up behind them. She heard herself mutter that all of it was so wretched, but then, as if for a moment lucid, she noticed that no one inside or outside the building was firing. The grisly figure of Packard, leading at a cautious pace, seemed ominous, like that of a reapeer carrying his scythe, with his gimpy walk, his loose, playful grip upon the gun. Bradley, carrying his gun the same way, as if to emulate the older man, seemed nevertheless childlike and simple.

"Look at that," she muttered over her shoulder, "look at that man."

"Packard?"

"Yes," she breathed, "look at him, and that bastard of a gun he's got."

"We shot them, too, Gretchin."

"I know. Did you look at them?"

"Yes."

As they approached the front of the building they could hear the chaotic scene unfolding. The mother was frantically holding her hands to her head and screaming.

"He took my boy! He's only ten years old!" she blubbered. "He took my boy!" Shaking violently, she retrieved a cigarette from the purse and tried to light it.

Amidst the confusion Bobbie Lee had mounted the motorcycle, turned the key, and was desperately repeatedly throwing her weight on the crank. Suddenly the engine rose from the grave, and she raised her chin and puffed her cheeks. Popping the shift down into first, she rode up to the mother and daughter. She looked at them, but said nothing, then turned to Connors and said to get on behind her.

As Connors got on, 9mm in hand, Bobbie Lee goosed the throttle and called over her shoulder, "If I lean forward, you lean forward. If I'm up, you're up, okay? Hug me and stay there."

"Isn't there a helmet?" asked Maggie, blotting a cut on her chin.

"Yeah," replied Bobbie Lee, her eyes glinting with mockery, "'cause it ain't safe."

"It isn't," Maggie pleaded.

Goosing the throttle, Bobbie Lee replied with a grin, "Horseshit."

Packard then stepped up to Connors and said, "Lady, you need a gun," and he drew the spare magnum from the jackass rig and presented its butt. As he took the nine from her and watched her hand close upon the magnum's grip he said to her, "Full metal. And remember, seven, not six."

Connors gave him a nod and Bobbie Lee throttled up and let out the clutch. At her command the Bonneville tore down the drive, turned onto the highway, and screamed away.

At seventy, Bobbie Lee molded herself to the tank and Connors, her left hand gripping Bobbie Lee's belt and her right the magnum, flattened herself in tandem. Their hair whipped mercilessly as the speedometer's needle crossed eighty, then ninety.

Minutes, very long minutes later they saw the car. It too was traveling well above seventy. As they approached the boy's face appeared at the back window. The man was yelling at him, and then reached back with the gun. The boy sat back down and the man turned back to his driving. As the motorcycle eased up behind them, the boy got up again and looked right into Bobbie Lee's eyes. Then she moved the Bonnie up just behind the car and pointed for him to get down. He stared at her for a second, then disappeared. Fiercely she pointed toward the right side of the back window and then bent down over the tank. Connors instantly raised the magnum and executed the long trigger pull as Bobbie Lee turned her face from the gun's cylinder gas. As the gun bucked and the right side of the rear window was blown in, Bobbie Lee raised herself and throttled forward, running up along the driver's side. The man, startled, had turned to see the hole as the Bonneville screamed forward. Now it was at the back left window, now at the man's own window. And now he turned and looked at his pursuers, his eyes wide, and Connors raised the magnum and fired twice through the glass into his face—*Blop! Blop!*—then four times through the blown-in window into his body—*Blam! Blam! Blam! Blam!*

Moving away from the car, Bobbie Lee throttled down and then simply followed the moribund hulk. The car's speed dropped to fifty, then to forty, then to thirty. Slowly the driverless car veered to the right and off the highway. It rolled along the gravel shoulder, then moved into the ditch and finally crashed against the circular end of a drainage pipe.

Bobbie Lee brought the Triumph up to the wrecked car, and Connors got off and looked inside for the boy. There was no need to look for the man, for she knew he had died with the first shots. Slowly the boy got up from the floor and peered at her.

"Hey, ked, are you hurt?" she said. But when he only stared at her, "Don't be scared, joost gat out." And pulling the door open, "Hope I dedn't shoot you." She took his arm and pulled him out.

"Hey there, boy," drawled Bobbie Lee, offering him a grin and giving the throttle a goose. "What's your name?"

"My name's Mark," he answered.

"I'm Bobbie Lee and this here's Killy, and we're pleased to meet you."

"Thank you, ma'am," he returned, looking at the motorcycle.

"Where you from, Mark?"

"Texas, right here. Where're you from, ma'am?"

"I'm from the great state of Tinnessee, boy."

"Well, Texas is a great state, too, it's the Lone Star State. We got the Alamo here."

"'We've got hills and grass, you ain't got nothin' but cactus an' dirt."

"Maybe, but I like it."

Connors, who had been checking the front seat, said, "That man's joost a poile of shet."

Bobbie Lee grinned again. "She means *pile of shit*, but she can't say it right 'cause she's from Irelan'."

"Okay," the boy said. "I've heard of that. I don't mind."

"Well," said Bobbie Lee, "at least she ain't no goddamn Yankee." Then she said, "Whyn't you git yoursilf up behind me here, Mark, we're gonna take you back to your mom."

Then he climbed up, got comfortable, and put his arms around her waist. "I'm glad I'm not dead," he said. "He was a bad man."

"Don't worry about et," returned Connors, getting up behind him, "the fucker's dead." And laying the magnum at his back, she put her arms around him to grip Bobbie Lee's belt.

Then Bobbie Lee shifted into first, throttled up, and let out the clutch. For a moment time stopped as she put the Bonnie into a graceful, sweeping U-turn. Then time started again as she straightened her up and brought them up to speed.

The boy, as if caught between two angels, at first hid his face. Then he opened his eyes and looked into the wind. Connors pressed close to hold him safe, but he did not mind. And Bobbie Lee's hair blew into his face, but he did not mind. He considered them both to be pretty, maybe like angels. And pressing his nose against Bobbie Lee's back, he considered her to smell good, maybe like the hills and grass of Tennessee.

Bobbie Lee eased the Bonneville to a soft stop in front of the mother and her daughter, then shut the engine down. Connors, clasped the magnum and got off, and the boy got off and threw his arms around his mother's waist. Bobbie Lee looked into the woman's eyes, then swung her leg off and dropped the kickstand.

"You'll prob'ly have to git another car," she said, "it's in a ditch with a bunch of bullet holes in it and a dead man on the floor of the front seat."

The woman, hugging her son, looked at Bobbie Lee, then at Connors, then at the magnum. "Good

Lord!" she muttered. "I'm jus' glad to have my son back. I was sure that man was gonna kill 'im. We only stopped here to ask if we could use the bathroom."

Stanley and Bradley had the SUVs waiting, engines at idle. They were both busy brushing out glass fragments from the second vehicle.

"Look at this thing," said Bradley with a sniff, "it's like a bomb site. I don't know how they're still alive."

"You should see what AK does to cars," the Russian replied. "Not like this. Much worse. One bullet goes through two doors."

Maggie, peering in, said, "Bradley, please be thorough. I don't want to sit in broken glass. What a mess."

Before getting into the first SUV, Connors handed the magnum back to Packard. "I'll have me peashooter back," she said.

He handed her the piece, then reloaded the .357 and stuffed it back into its holster. "Lady," he rasped, walking away, "get a gun."

Climbing in beside Bobbie Lee, Connors put her head back against the rest and closed her eyes.

Martina said from the front seat, "That's quite a motorcycle."

Connors gave a shrug, her eyes still closed. "Et's Bretish, but at least et got us there, t'anks to t'is girl here."

Bobbie Lee winced. "What's wrong with it bein' British? You Irish and your thing aginst Inglan', it's a little unreasonable sometimes."

With her eyes still closed, "No more than yours es against Yankees."

"Ah, come on, don't git me started. This ain't about politics. Triumph's a good motorcycle. A little shitty on the ignition system, but not much else wrong with 'em, long as you carry a wrinch with you. Besides, we caught the bastard, didn't we? So, bow the knee, show some respict, girl."

Martina, who had been on her phone, lowered her window and said out to the mother, "The Waco police are en route and should be here any minute. We'll wait until they show up, then leave. Is that all right?"

"That's fine."

Martina looked at the boy. "You look like you've had a motorcycle ride. What's your name?"

"My name's Mark, ma'am."

And to the girl, "What's yours?"

"Jenny. I'm twelve."

Martina merely smiled. The girl's eyes looked like her own, she thought. She could almost see Papa and her sisters as they drove through the night from East Germany, and almost feel the cold as it closed around them. Which was certainly the opposite, she mused, of this awful Texas heat. She recalled how her stomach had hurt with anxiety as she watched Papa pour gasoline from the glass jug into the car's tank, and how it had hurt even more as she watched him wither as his homeland slipped away from him forever.

"Here they come now," she said, her eyes on the police car coming up the drive. Then she smiled again at the boy and girl. "My name's Martina."

The woman, pulling her children close, watched until the SUVs were on the highway, then gave them a wave and turned to address the officer.

At the motor inn the team went to work packing, cleaning up, and then loading the SUVs. Maggie, who had been on the phone with Kessler, announced that the plane had been refueled and was waiting for them.

Pulling the door to their room closed, Martina thought of Ted and of how he would be pleased to find only their keys left in their rooms. Then she got into the SUV, and Stanley drove to the highway and accelerated. Turning her visor down, she checked its mirror for the other SUV, then flipped it back into place. She knew that Bradley and Gretchin would be bickering.

At the airport, the same sedan sat idling beside the plane. A window was down and the same three men were chatting with the same pilot. As the SUVs approached they got out and in unison pulled their ball caps on.

After the Otter was loaded and the team had climbed in and buckled up, Maggie automatically closed her eyes in preparation for takeoff. Then oddly she heard the voice of Packard from behind her telling her not to worry, so she opened her eyes and put a hand up to signal she was all right. But he was not convinced and offered to shoot the pilot if they crashed. Then she gave a laugh and reported that really she was all set for the trip. She was glad for his concern and for the first time thought him to be charming. A minute later the pilot had the plane turned around and lined up.

Then everything vibrated and she felt the acceleration. For a moment she laughed to herself, for if Bradley had sat next to her he would be telling her about the Pratt and Whitneys. Moments later they were up and she looked through her window to see a Texas landscape bathed in a Texas sunshine. Facing forward, she closed her eyes again, but this time in relief, as the plane continued its ascent to cruising altitude.

The return flight to Philadelphia, less stressful than the flight out, gave Martina a chance to consider the Agency's offer to relocate the team to the farm. It was a grand proposal, she thought, one that could easily fail. What would the isolation do to Gretchin, for instance, induce her to sleep with Bradley? And what could result from that, a suicide, a murder? She wondered why life seemed so bent on mixing things up for those who wished only to live in peace. She winced at her use of the term *peace*, for its application to those who had just completed a campaign of violent death seemed ironic to the point of being ludicrous. *Live in peace*, what was that? What in God's name did that even mean anymore? Then she thought of the victims and the criminals. If some people could blur the difference between the two, she could not. And if her life had a purpose, it must be a moral one. The gray areas of life were significant, to be sure. Indeed, at times, they were huge, making the truth difficult to discern. But if everything were gray, the truth would be nonexistent and life would be meaningless, and she, for one, could not live a life without meaning.

When they landed at the airport near Philadelphia, the grogginess set in again. It was like the flu, a virus that seemed determined to affect every creature passing within its circle.

"You are a very tired woman," Stanley observed, helping her from the plane. "We are needing to get you home to bed."

"And you can rub my back," she said. "I need to sleep in my own bed. I need you there, as you always are, but in our own bed."

CHAPTER 17

Philadelphia

"I'm a city girl," protested Gretchin, visiting one evening for dinner. "I'm going to find it hard to grow spuds. I mean, what happens to my Fellini and pizza and art? I can't think slow, I just can't."

Martina put her hands together, but then brought them apart again, for too often she had seen Kessler make the gesture. "I don't know," she replied. "I've been thinking a lot about it myself, but I have no idea what to say to Paul, at this point anyway."

Stanley, finishing his wine, held the glass up and looked at it. "We could all move to Moscow," he offered.

"And do what, my American husband, hang your cowboy boots on Lenin's ears? It's funny how you can be so Russian when we're here and yet so American when we go there."

He shrugged. "This inconsistency is human."

After listening to them, Gretchin said, "When I look at you two, I realize that's a little bit what I want."

Martina wrinkled her nose. "What?"

"That adversarial stuff. You know, the exchange you two have. I want that."

"Gretchin, you have nothing *but* the adversarial."

"I know, I know, people say that. But I mean with a husband and in my own family. I want that arena. I want a husband, I want to be married and I want—"

"What?" Martina interrupted, "children?"

"No, of course not. I know I'm too old, I understand that, but I could adopt."

"And that's realistic?"

"Maybe not. I guess I'm not the type to be scooting around after little kids. But I would like a household, what's wrong with that? I would like to get up in the morning, screw my husband, have breakfast, and then maybe just do art, or whatever, but I would like to have it all as part of a household." When the other simply sighed, she said, "Maybe that's not being realistic. But were you and Stanley being realistic when you fell in love?" And when there was no reply, she continued, "Love is real, and wanting it is being realistic. Wanting a husband, a family, wanting anything real is being realistic."

"I'm not sure I agree with that logic. But what you're really asking, I think, is how any of that could happen if you moved to an isolated place like a farm and simply continued to work for the Agency."

"Something like that."

Martina looked at her for a moment. "How are the cuts to your face and neck healing?"

"I'm okay, I was just peppered."

"You were lucky."

"I know. And it gave me a fresh sense of how ephemeral life is and how I've lost my youth."

"Youth, Gretchin, really? That's such a relative term."

"But it means something real."

A sigh. "Yes, it does. Mine was gone, but still I fell in love."

"And you married too."

Leaning back in her chair, Martina instinctively reached out for Stanley's hand, gave it a squeeze, then released it. "I'm inclined to think that, unless it's done right, moving to a remote facility could practically ruin all of us."

"We're not computers," said Gretchin. "They can't just take us and plug us in somewhere else."

"They cannot do it," said the Russian, "and also expect us to be human and creative. They have to pick one. I think they would pick for us to have the human and creative side, because that is what they are exploiting in us. They are doing it for good, yes?"

The women looked at each other.

"That's the theory," replied Martina.

He smiled at them. "They are using our humanness to do inhumane things to humans for the good of humanity. Everything is right, until it is not. Everything is correct, until it is not. Everything is constant, until it is not."

Martina returned the smile. "You are making me uncomfortable, Mr. Osipov."

"Only fools," he replied, "are comfortable."

October was nearly over when Kessler came again to meet with the team. He arrived with a sidekick, and they sat together on the couch graciously praising Maggie for the tea and cookies. Kessler seemed especially jovial.

"It's chilly out," he offered, smiling around at them all. He did not like having to manage a cup and saucer. He did not like having to do perfunctory things to achieve a simple end. And what was it with the cookies? Every time he visited he got tea in a cup and saucer and cookies to balance and eat.

"Another cookie, Paul?" queried Maggie pleasantly.

He looked at her. "Thank you, Maggie, yes, of course, I would love one, thanks." Carefully he chose one from the tray, bit into it, and then smiled at her. "This is very good, they are always very good, just delicious."

"Oh, take two."

"Of course, yes, thank you. That way, I won't have to keep asking you for them." Now he had the extra cookie to balance on the saucer. God, the bullshit he had to wade through just to get people to do what he wanted them to.

He looked around at them, this team of his. God, what a peculiar slice of humanity! What exactly did this cookie-pushing Maggie want out of life, he wondered? And Martina, sixty-nine years old and so in love that it was obscene. And

Connors, well, here was someone he would never understand. How many scarred-over bullet holes did she have, how many residual lead fragments did she bear? What she wanted out of life was anybody's guess. How could a woman with hair like that, a face as beautiful as that, a body as well formed as that, be such an executioner? How could God go so wrong in making such a piece of work? And what should he say about the rest, the psychotic Packard, the sensitive Osipov, the neurotic Gretchin, the crazy Henry woman? Of the bunch of them, the only one he could call normal would be Bradley.

"Paul," offered Bradley, his tone almost pastoral, "try the coffee, if you don't like the tea."

"Bradley," said Gretchin, "stick a sock in it, okay?"

"Why?" he returned. "What's wrong with that?"

"You were born with both your feet all the way in your mouth."

With a sneer, "And you were born with a torch for a tongue. Know what you are? You're pathologically critical."

"Oh, that's a big word for you, Bradley, I'll bet you read up on it."

"I did."

"And so now, what, you're a goddamn psychiatrist?"

Kessler quickly cleared his throat. "Uh, well, yes, here we all are again. I wanted to talk to everyone tonight about the relocation. I would guess you've been thinking about it. Any ideas?"

Martina scratched her chin. "Actually, yes."

"Please."

"I think, Paul, for us, and I think I speak for all of us, it comes down to this. Relocation does seem to make sense, but not to a place as far away and remote as the farm in Vermont. Taking the complaints and suggestions as I've heard them, I would suggest a compromise."

"And that would be?" he queried cautiously.

"Some place, and it can be a farm or whatever, in rural Pennsylvania, would do very well. In the Lancaster area there might be an estate or old farm that could work. The developments or newer areas might prove problematic, since they would be more likely to fall under the scrutiny of neighborhood association-type groups. But an older estate or property could be developed for our purposes, I would think. And it would be near Harrisburg and even Philadelphia for culture."

"Ah," he exclaimed, "it would be in Amish country. That's brilliant, excellent, a great idea. How does that sound to everybody else?"

Momentarily Gretchin said, "It sounds good to me. I have to be near a city, any city. As with everyone else here, my cover is genuine. I'm an artist, I draw, I paint, I need to look at other art sometimes. I need culture, even if it means simply going out to a movie occasionally, and I don't mean to the local movie house in Podunk."

Maggie chimed, "I'm good with it, too."

As the idea was found acceptable by the entire team, Kessler could hardly contain his enthusiasm. He said he felt certain that the proposal should have little difficulty passing successfully under the scrutiny of the Agency.

"That's great," he said brightly, "you've done my job for me, Martina. Good work."

She looked back at him, at his mouth as he munched his cookie and pretended to be enjoying himself. She watched as his eyes went over them all as though making a count of his toy soldiers. She thought of the gun in her purse, the war implement she had fired in this man's service. But then, had it been so? Had she leveled and fired the .38 in this man's service? Had she led the team into a battle this man alone had created? Had they all gone to war for this lord? Life was malicious, she thought as she looked at him, this pitiless lord. Oh, he was full of mercy and sympathy when he wanted to reach to the center of your being, and of praise when he wanted to capture you and enlist you in his army. But what he used you for was service that could not countenance pity. And through it all he simply smiled at you, as if agreeing with you. Was this really a man, or was it a dragon? Did it walk, or creep and crawl and fly about? Was that skin or scales? And beyond that smile, would you find a man with a decent heart, or a dragon with a burned soul?

It was a good analogy, she thought. But then a pang corrected her, as though Gretchin had whispered in her ear that such an analogy was inappropriate, that, as everyone knew, there were dragons who were more decent than men.

CHAPTER 18

Lancaster County, Pennsylvania, Spring 2010

It was in the spring that relocation was finalized. Martina's suggestion had been forwarded by Kessler and approved by the Agency. An estate of eighty acres was located by Martina and Maggie, purchased by the Agency, and renovated by private contractors. Along with two old stone houses, the property included a six-car garage that had been converted from a riding stable, two wells, and a stream that ran the length of the tract. The property, somewhat secluded, was located in the area Martina had suggested.

"How does it feel, dear?" queried Maggie, lifting her water glass. "We're here now, all of us, including the two new dears." With her free hand, she patted the head of Helga, who preened at the attention. "Isn't she a wonderful dog?"

The team, seated around the dining room's massive square table, all turned to look at the dog.

"She is, yes," replied Martina.

"And as to my first question?"

"I feel pretty good about it. Nothing's perfect, but this is close. We're here, we're all alive and well. I hope it will stay that way, but I admit it's a dubious hope to buy into."

"That's kind of negative," Bradley said.

Gretchin leaned her head to the side. "Yeah," she said, "he doesn't want you to be negative, he got to keep his Corvette. And what more could there be to a full life than a gun and a car? Oh, I'm sorry, not just a car, a Corvette. Full macho credit here."

He mimicked her head movement. "It fits very nicely in the garage, if I say so myself. I should be able to keep it. Why should I have to give it up?"

"Because it's an expensive, ostentatious trinket of your egocentric little mind?"

"You're pretty self-centered, Gretchin, anybody can see that from your tattoo. I'm not sure you should be throwing stones."

Grabbing her napkin and wadding it up, "God, what an infant you are. A tattoo says I'm self-centered, but a gaudy Corvette doesn't say you are?"

Stretching his legs under the table, he replied mockingly, "I'm just saying, Gretchin, I mean, every time I look at you I see that dragon crawling across your neck, like you're saying, *look at me, look at me, I'm trying to catch your eye.*"

She took her fork and pointed it at him. "I may have to work with you, but I am infinitely grateful that I don't have to live in the same house."

Packard grunted, "So are we. You two are nuts."

The estate's two residential structures formed an L and were connected by an enclosed walkway. Both houses, double-storied, with airy attics and cool, dry cellars, faced a driveway that encircled a stone fountain. Maggie called the fountain a birdbath, since it did not work and only collected rainwater. On the first floor of the larger house, which Stanley called The Big House, were located the living room, dining room, and kitchen. The first floor of the smaller house, which Bradley called The Den, provided the team with two recreation rooms, a tiny library, and a spacious reading room. Martina and Stanley, Maggie, Gretchin, and Connors had taken bedrooms for themselves in The Big House, while Bradley, Packard, and Bobbie Lee had chosen bedrooms in The Den.

Connors reached for a wedge of cantaloupe. "Yous two foight all the toime. Et's pratty hard on the rast of us."

"Yes," said Martina cheerily, hoping to refocus the discussion, "it's working out quite well. Paul said they were even putting in a shooting range this week. Isn't that exciting? Stanley, what do you think?"

Taking a moment to push back from the table, "This is very good. KGB did not get this kind of thing."

Bradley pointed a finger at him. "That's America, pal."

"Bradley, please don't," said Gretchin.

"Well," said Maggie brightly, "isn't this nice. We have a new facility, which we all like, and two wonderful new dogs, aren't they lovely? Tomorrow I'm taking them for a walk around the property."

"Be careful," said Bradley, "this is a big place. Eighty acres, try to wrap your head around that. That's going to be a hike, take a water bottle." Then he added, pointing his finger at her, "Don't forget what Paul said, nobody's supposed to go anywhere unarmed."

Maggie, who did not appreciate being pointed at, returned, "Bradley, what would we do without you? Thank you for reminding me, but I will have these two."

"And a gun," he said.

"I totally agree," said Stanley, pushing back to balance on the chair, "no one should be getting lazy. I could tell you stories, but I will not do it. Every criminal has a friend or a brother or whatever, and people never forget. Eventually it will be happening, people will be coming after us. Right now my back is killing me, because I am leaning against Tokarev. But if someone comes through door, I do not have to be asking them to wait until I go up the stairs for my pistol. Would you like KGB stories? I can give you examples."

"Please, Osipov," said Bradley, "I'm tired of hearing about your Commie friends. No stories."

Martina looked at her husband. "You shouldn't lean back in your chair like that. It weakens the legs. And anyway, who's dumb enough to do it with a gun across his backbone?"

From a dark corner two eyes met Maggie's, and she called softly, "Hey, Tai Ping."

When Kessler had recommended that two or three dogs be acquired to help with the grounds, the team responded by appointing Bobbie Lee and Connors to find the most appropriate dogs. The purebred German Shepherd, returned to her breeder to be put to sleep for killing a prize rooster and nipping at a boy was adopted and given the name Helga. The strange, lanky Jindo-Chow, unwanted because of his fierceness, was chosen from a Philadelphia shelter and given the name Tai Ping.

Martina, considering the serious Helga, then the formidable Tai Ping, said to Maggie, "I think you should be quite safe going for a walk with these two. Except that Tai Ping doesn't seem to want to bark. He hasn't made a sound yet."

"And he prob'ly won't," said Bobbie Lee, coming in from the kitchen. "They said he was real quiet, kinda barkless. He's the opposite of the shepherd, I guess. Helga barks like a field gun. Bet I could hear her half a mile away. But Mr. Ping here, I don't know, I've heard him bay, but not bark. That's one scary dog."

"God, he's a brute," said Gretchin, swallowing. "Why, again, are we calling him Tai Ping?"

Bobbie Lee set a pie on the table and licked her finger. "In Chinese it means *great peace*. It's supposed to give the idea of *peace and security*." She threw a glance in the dog's direction. "Tell y'all what. If I was gonna rob this here place and I spied that there dog, either of these dogs, lit alone both of 'em prowlin' around, I'd pick another house, sure would. Even a magnum wouldn't do me any good. Have y'all seen these dogs run? Yep, I'd jus' turn around an' leave. An' I'd tip-toe away, yep."

"And again, the name Helga," queried Gretchin, "means what?"

"It's gotta Scandinavian origin. It means *holy*. Me an' Killy thought it sounded real nice."

Gretchin's eyebrows rose. "Holy?"

It was Connors who answered. "Aye, holy loike the angels, guardian angels."

Printed in April 2019
by Rotomail Italia S.p.A., Vignate (MI) - Italy